TACTICAL RESPONSE TEAM — BOOK ONE
FIGHTER

CINDY BONDS

Scrivenings PRESS
Quench your thirst for story.
www.ScriveningsPress.com

But one thing I do: forgetting what lies behind and straining forward to what lies ahead.
Philippians 3:13b (ESV)

Copyright © 2021 by Cindy Bonds

Published by Scrivenings Press LLC
15 Lucky Lane
Morrilton, Arkansas 72110
https://ScriveningsPress.com

Printed in the United States of America

All rights reserved. No part of this publication may be reproduced, stored in a retrieval system, or transmitted in any form or by any means—for example, electronic, photocopy and recording— without the prior written permission of the publisher. The only exception is brief quotation in printed reviews.

Paperback ISBN 978-1-64917-161-0

eBook ISBN 978-1-64917-162-7

Library of Congress Control Number: 2021948010

Scripture quotations are from The ESV® Bible (The Holy Bible, English Standard Version®), copyright © 2001 by Crossway, a publishing ministry of Good News Publishers. Used by permission. All rights reserved.

Editors: Elena Hill and K. Banks

Cover by Linda Fulkerson, bookmarketinggraphics.com

All characters are fictional, and any resemblance to real people, either factual or historical, is purely coincidental.

PROLOGUE

"So, what'd they do to get asylum?"

Lieutenant Evan Mitchell frowned at Sergeant Rogers. "Not our concern. We just follow orders, Sergeant."

"Yes, sir."

Glancing at the trio walking ahead of him, he wondered the same thing.

The couple had a woman with them. She had to be older and, from the way she held her head, appeared unfazed by the danger. A younger woman would be terrified to see men with guns raid their compound and escort them out of town.

But she seemed unaffected. Covered in a burka, only her eyes showed in the dim light. They looked determined.

Whoever they were, the U.S. government deemed them worthy of a SEAL team escort to American soil. They had executed the entry without a hitch. If they could just get to the extraction point without trouble ...

As they approached the helipad, Evan turned. That overwhelming feeling that had saved him and his team in the past told him they needed cover. Now.

A glint on the hillside three clicks away caught his attention. "Down! Everyone down!"

The tremendous wave threw him backward. His body slammed into a Humvee, knocking the wind from his lungs. Burning remnants of an assault vehicle sat in front of him, and the smell of sulfur was thick in the air.

"Lieutenant!"

Evan gulped air. "Protect the bird! Get them out of here!"

Small arms fire erupted. He righted himself and rushed to the defensive. Straining to see through blurred vision, he fired on the insurgents. The sound of another shell whistled through the air.

"Down!"

His team took cover just as the blast shook the ground. The roar of rotor blades drowned out the shouts and gunfire. Evan dove behind a vehicle and sprayed suppressive fire while the helicopter lifted and banked away.

"Sir? Where's the evac?"

"They'll be here! Stay at your position!"

The small arms fire ceased as the helicopter disappeared into the darkness. Evan steadied himself from his position behind a vehicle and sucked in a deep breath, still shaky from the blast's impact.

"Sir?" Someone grabbed his arm.

Spots appeared. A wave of dizziness sent Evan to his knees.

The echoing sound of Rogers's voice rolled through his head as his world collapsed and went dark.

1

Two Years Later

The murmur of low voices hummed throughout the large building. The smell of diesel and oil filled his senses as he paced. What was taking so long? They'd been in this dreadful place a week—biding his time and making plans.

The men who filled the room were all hired hands. If he were home instead of the United States, he would get rid of every one of them and employ a new team. Scanning their faces, his jaw clenched.

Which one would betray him? There was always one.

"We're ready, sir."

He glared at the militant man in front of him. "You and your men will do everything I say, complete this job without fail. Do you understand me? It's not just your payment for the job on the line." He gritted his teeth as the man nodded.

He'd spent years searching, buying confidences and lives, anything to get him the information needed. Now that they were so close, he couldn't fail. That's why he was here. He could only trust himself to complete the mission.

He would get what he wanted. Revenge and reconciliation would be his. No one would stop him.

2

"Seriously, Bex? You're not going to fight it?"

Bexley Bowers sighed into the phone as she roamed Dallas's large downtown mall. "Reggie, there's nothing to fight. Our contract specifically states no personal liaisons between coworkers."

Reggie huffed. "Yeah, well, it's not like you two were actual coworkers. He's about as high up as he can get. He just didn't want you to tell everyone what a jerk he is."

Bexley chuckled, pausing to window shop the boutique clothes. "I'm good, really."

"I don't believe that for a second."

Ignoring her badgering friend, Bexley continued. "I'll land on my feet, Regg. I always do."

"Okay, if you say so." Reggie sighed. "I've got to go. It's getting to that time of year, and we're trying to work out a schedule for holiday travel. Just think, now you can have a life instead of flying around to different lands protecting a bunch of rich people who don't want protection."

Bexley forced out a chuckle. "Yeah, lucky me. Take care."

"See you when I see you."

The call ended, and Bexley shoved the phone in her pocket.

Sure. It was easy to have a life now that she had lost her job, the one thing that had grounded her all these years.

With a grunt, she pushed forward down the east wing of the mall. Just because her reputation was ruined and her future empty didn't mean she was completely without. She had her health—that was something, right?

Several interviews and a part-time job later, here she was, clinging to her foundations as they seemed to crumble yet again. With her life in ruins, there had to be something more. Hence the trip to the bookstore.

The smell of freshly baked cookies and salty pretzels filled the air, and her stomach growled. Finding the bookstore needed to happen sooner rather than later, or she'd find herself in front of the cookie counter. And that would be an unbelievably bad idea.

Man, cookies ...

Stepping through the opened storefront, Bex gazed across the bookstore. Two women in the aisle in front of her looking over a book, a man to the left on the phone. Her jaw clenched. Being alert and watchful had been her previous job description. Now a part-time librarian, she didn't need to keep noticing every single person, exit, and thoroughfare when entering a room.

As she studied the different genres, her mind shifted. Hopefully, something here would lift her spirits, give her a better focus. After all, she now had the time to find a new path, maybe even a new career.

Standing in the self-help section, she browsed the titles, frowning at all the misnamed masterpieces. *Finding Yourself, Finding Your Inner Peace, Finding ...*

With a sigh, she paused. Her pulse quickened, her skin pricked. Years of training told her she was being watched. Cutting her eyes, she saw an empty aisle.

Let it go.

It would be harder than anticipated to accept she was no longer on protection detail, no longer a special operations agent.

Navigating to the Christian section, she perused the covers and titles. It wasn't that she didn't believe in God, but He seemed to be silent in her life, leaving her frustrated, alone, and needing to fill those missing pieces. She halted with her hand on a book and peered over her shoulder.

Once more, nothing.

Focus.

Shrugging off past instincts, she fixed her attention on each cover. Finally deciding on a daily devotional that wouldn't take hours of concentration, she started toward the registers. As she paused in the aisle to glance at her book, someone plowed into her from behind.

She spun. A tall, lanky man stared at her.

"I'm sorry, am I in your way?" Her tone came out more heated than intended, her frustration getting the best of her.

"Actually, yes," he sneered.

The smell of cigar smoke and alcohol wafted from him. Her nose wrinkled.

"Problem?" A voice boomed from behind the smelly man.

Her assailant turned to a man in khaki pants and a green polo.

"No," he mumbled.

As the offender turned, a large bulge on his side underneath his long coat became visible. Bexley's uneasiness jumped up. Here in the heart of Texas, the end of October didn't require a jacket, much less a coat.

"You okay?" The man intervening looked past the smelly man to her, his eyes peering from underneath the bill of his hat.

Based on stance and hairstyle, she suspected military. From the tattoo barely visible from under the shirt sleeve, she assumed Navy.

"I'm fine." She nodded at the bulge in the man's long coat before locking eyes with the Navy man.

Navy's eyes narrowed on the smelly man. Bexley turned, dropping the book on the stack and heading for the exit. A force yanked her arm back, and she reactively swung. Pain radiated down her hand as she landed a blow to her assailant's face. The man stumbled backward with a grunt.

Her arm free, she shook out her hand and attempted to leave again. A burly, bearded man stood at the doors, a semi-automatic rifle across his chest.

"You!" Her aggressor yelled, seizing her hair. Her head jerked back as she twisted, attempting to free herself from his grip.

"Stop!"

Navy's order sounded as she fell. Instead of slamming to the ground, Navy pulled her up to safety.

"Easy, man." Navy protectively pushed her behind him, holding one hand up in the air while he gripped her side.

"Give me your weapons." Her attacker aimed his rifle at the two of them, wiping the dark, red liquid as it ran from his nose.

Navy carefully pulled a gun from his waist.

"The ankle too."

Pulling up his khakis, he unsheathed another gun from his ankle.

"Now, move." He fired off a few rounds into the ceiling, creating screams of panic throughout the large store.

She turned and followed the crowd, pulling her purse in tightly, hoping they wouldn't take it.

"Just do as they say," Navy spoke calmly into her ear as he pushed at her waist, guiding her amidst the chaotic scene of people crying and wailing.

"Phones in the bag!" The bearded man from the door now stood in front of them with a bag.

She shoved hers inside, then followed the throng from the bookstore into a small breakroom.

As they entered, a man dressed in black aimed his rifle, motioning them against the wall.

"You, come here." Turning, her attacker grabbed Navy's arm, shoving the rifle barrel in his face. "Sit." He pushed Navy down to the floor as she was guided to the other side. Squeezing between an older couple and some teenagers, she slid to the floor. "Quiet. I want quiet!"

Glancing at her, her assailant spat blood on the floor before marching out of the room, the bearded man in tow. An audible lock echoed, leaving one man to guard the twenty or so hostages now trapped.

Scanning the room, Bexley rubbed her pained fist, shoving her purse out of view. The best exit was the fire door at the far end of the workroom. The sign hung down from the ceiling, but she couldn't see the door. This bookstore sat on the bottom floor of the three-story mall, the east side. That exit would lead them outside to where she always parked.

Counting heads, she studied those sitting in the room. A mother with two children sat across from her, four teenage girls sat to her left, holding hands and crying. The mix included several women who had to be closer to sixty and the older couple, the manager, and three other employees based on their vests and nametags.

Feeling the hair on her neck stand on end, her gaze filtered through the group and found Navy watching her intently. Once the abductor turned his focus, she rested her hand on her purse, making a gun with her finger and thumb. He nodded, a slight grin forming on his lips.

Taking a second to work herself up, she loudly wailed, "We're all going to die!" Burying her head in her hands, her body trembled and shook.

"Shut up!"

"I'm so scared. What if I never make it home?"

"I said quiet!" Their guard rushed over and kicked at her side a few times, making her wince as pain radiated through her ribs. She curled up in a ball against the wall to protect herself

The girls to her left shushed her, letting out their own whimpers.

"Hey, let me see if I can calm her down." Navy's voice sounded over her fake sobs still echoing in the room.

"Fine, just shut her up."

In an instant, Navy appeared, pulling her up in his arms. Her knees lay across his lap as she gripped his shirt and pushed her face into his chest.

"It's going to be okay, calm down." His soothing voice and gentle touch gave her goosebumps. Ignoring her reaction, she diminished her wails to a soft sob. "Good, just take a deep breath."

She did so, keeping her face turned into him. Listening for the guard, she squinted, his back to them as he paced. Leaning forward slightly, her eyes locked with Navy's deep blues.

"You'll have to chamber it," she mouthed as he gave her a wink.

She didn't even hear him unzip the handbag to pull the gun free, but the weight lifted from the strap.

"Distraction?"

He frowned and shook his head slightly.

Scowling, she leaned back against him, hoping to keep his arm hidden as his other arm stretched across her body to grip her shoulder. They needed something to get the abductor's attention, some way to throw him off so that gun he had aimed at the crowd didn't inadvertently fire.

The manager caught her gaze and nodded. Footsteps halted behind her. Wiping her face, she turned. The guard stood there staring.

"You, move away." He pointed his weapon, motioning, then glowered as her lip lowered to a full pout. "Don't even think about it."

With the rifle trained on her, she paused her routine, then felt Navy squeeze her shoulder.

Fighter

"She might keep quiet if you point that gun away for a second." Navy's calm voice sounded.

The guard aimed the rifle up toward the ceiling, "Fine, better?"

She nodded and felt the tap on her back.

"I ... I'll scoot over, okay?"

The guard frowned, nodding as her body eased away from Navy. A single gunshot rang out, and their captor collapsed on the floor.

Navy leaped to his feet. "Everyone out the fire exit," he yelled, aiming the gun at the main door for cover.

Bodies rose and shuffled to the exit as she jumped up and helped the woman next to her stand.

"Help her," Bexley snagged the manager's arm.

The man took hold of the elderly woman and headed for the fire exit. Relieving the now dead man of his weapon, Bexley kept her aim at the door, sliding over to Navy.

"Here, trade me." She handed the rifle over and waited for her gun, but he tucked it into his waistband.

"You need to go, now." He started firing at the storeroom door as it cracked open.

"I'm not leaving you here alone."

"This is my job. Get out of here!"

Finding another weapon on the man lying dead on the floor, she ignored the sight of his blood seeping into the carpet.

"Get out. That's an order."

"I'm not a soldier, and you're not doing this on your own," she muttered, going to a knee and taking aim.

Bullets pounded through the storeroom door as Navy tackled her to the ground, covering her and rolling her toward the wall.

"Get off." She pushed at him.

"Then stay down," he bit out as he jumped up to return fire.

A man burst through, but Navy had him down in a second, then flipped over a table for cover while gunshots rang out. Sitting up against the wall, she waited for the gunfire to ease.

"I'll get the guy, you cover me," she called over her shoulder.

"What? No, get out of here," he yelled as he sent another round of bullets through the door.

Wasting no time, she charged the doorway and pulled the now deceased attacker through, ignoring the sounds of the gunfire. Staying low, Bexley pulled a grenade from the man's waist and threw it into the main bookstore through the door.

One more yank had the deceased man's legs free, the door to the bookstore finally shutting. Smoke filtered through the cracks. As she stood, someone gripped her arm and she swung again, missing the target.

"What the ..."

Two men stood behind her in tactical gear, both wearing khakis and green polos underneath armored vests.

One man eased off his rifle, frowning over her shoulder. "Evan?"

Navy rose to his feet, fuming, his face and neck red as he stomped in front of her. "I told you to leave."

"Ev."

"And I told you I'm not a soldier. You don't give me orders."

His cobalt eyes seared into hers. "Just because you think you can fight—"

"Think? Don't push it, Navy."

Her tone fell flat, the adrenaline of the situation falling on her shoulders and chest, making her want to either punch something or pass out.

"Evan, we've got to go."

Navy pushed into her space again. "Get. Out. Now."

"Then give. Me. My. Gun." She fisted her hands and straightened her shoulders, not willing to leave her grandfather's pistol behind.

"I can't." He broke his gaze long enough to nod to the men behind her. "Take her outside."

"Actually, he wants all of us out there right now. We need to discuss the situation. The building is far from secure."

Navy's friend spoke up as the second guy stood motionless, his gun aimed at the storeroom door.

"Fine. Let's go."

As they headed to the exit, several armed men rushed past them, wearing vests that read SWAT. Navy pushed on her waist to get her out the exit door, stepping into the bright sunshine amid the chaos of officers and armed personnel roaming the lot.

3

Evan's temper flared as he directed the woman to their command center van. Guiding her up the steps and inside, Sergio looked up at him from the computer.

"Get out."

Sergio cut back and forth between him and the woman, then nodded and high-tailed it out as she paced the narrow space.

Throwing his hat down, he sat in a chair so he wouldn't have to lean his body over in the small vehicle.

His eyes followed her as she paced. "What're you doing?"

"Right now? Trying to keep from passing out."

The sarcasm in her tone annoyed him, but he saw right through it.

"Sit down before you do."

"I'm fine." She glared as she continued her two-step back and forth at the widest part of the vehicle. "I thought you had to talk to someone?"

"He can wait. What's your name?"

"You first."

Ignoring him, she kept her right hand wrapped around her waist.

"Sit before you pass out. I'm assuming you wouldn't want me picking you up off the floor."

She frowned and shook her head.

"My name is Evan Mitchell." Biting back his pride, he gave her the concession. "I work for the TRT. Tactical Rescue Team."

"I know what it is." She rolled her eyes as her pacing ended, and she leaned up against the wall separating the cab from the back.

Sliding slowly down, she grimaced and let out a breath.

"Hey. Hey? Give me your name." He jumped down to his knees to assess her injuries as her eyes closed and her head leaned back.

"Bex ... Bexley Bowers," she muttered.

"Okay, Bexley, let me see your side."

"It's just bruised." Her voice sounded hoarse as she shook her head, gripping her shirt and tensing up.

"Your hand then, I'm pretty sure you've done something—"

"I'm fine." Her voice came back strong, her big green eyes looking up into his as she yanked her hand away.

"You sure are stubborn," he grunted, working hard to keep from yelling as he sat back on his heels. "Look, you need to be checked out. So, either way, you'll be seen."

"Fine, I'll deal with the paramedics. Send 'em in. I know you have somewhere else to be." The control had come back to her voice as she focused on him, a flash of fire intensified in her bright green eyes.

"You won't be allowed to leave, just so you know." He stood and grabbed his hat from the floor, stomping to the entrance before he paused. "And try to keep from hitting anyone else while you're at it," he shouted as he made his way down the stairs and slammed the door.

Marching up to his team, he shook his head.

"Have a pleasant conversation?" His teammate Danica Freeman looked up at him with a smirk, fueling his rage even more.

Fighter

"Drop it." His glare had her nodding. "What do we have?"

"What about her?" Buck Thompson, his team leader, nodded to the van. "She need help?"

"Yeah, but she's not letting anyone near her so, just let her sit."

Jeff held out a hand. "Easy there, tiger, if she needs help—"

"She'll get it, Jeff." Evan snapped as the rest of the team stood in silence.

"A word, Evan." Buck motioned as he was pulled from the group, following his boss and mentor out of earshot from the others. "Okay, I need to know what happened and why you're so ... angry."

"Why?" Evan thrust his hand in the van's direction. "She wouldn't leave the scene. She moved into gunfire to retrieve one of the attacker's bodies." He seethed that no one else seemed to notice how infuriating and bull-headed that woman was being.

"Why do you suppose she would do that?" Buck's calmness only irritated him more.

"I don't know, why don't you go ask her?" He held back a grimace.

Buck only crossed his arms, his wide stance impatient.

Evan released a breath, flexing his hands at his sides. "I guess to get the door closed. The body was blocking it from closing."

"Anything else?" Buck raised his eyebrow.

"I don't know. Maybe so we could ID him, if that kind of thing were even going through her head." He doubted it; she was probably just trying to find a way to close off the room again. "She said she wouldn't leave me alone to fight."

"Okay, so she's got a head on her shoulders."

His mouth dropped. "What? She put both of us at risk. She's a danger—"

Buck held his hand up, and Evan clamped his jaw shut. Easing his breathing, he waited. Buck was the most patient and intense man he'd ever met. Buck's lifetime of field experience and training as a Ranger trumped Evan's five-year stint as a

SEAL. The man had nerves of steel and was the only reason he had joined this little outfit in the first place.

"Evan, start thinking clearly. She was scared ..."

"Nope, you're wrong about that one. I'm pretty sure she didn't have one fear rolling through her the whole time."

Buck raised his eyebrow. "So, you're saying she seemed in control?"

Evan nodded.

"From what I've gathered, her weapon was what you used to get out?"

"Yeah, her weapon, her distraction. The guy got in a few good hits to her side ..." Evan trailed off, clearing his throat at the last part. Glancing at the van, he rubbed the back of his neck. Between her side and hand, she was probably hurting.

"Now that you've thought it over and calmed, let's get an action plan together."

"Yes, sir."

Returning to the group, the other four members stood ready for action.

"Update?" Buck motioned to Jeff for a sitrep.

"From what we've been told, a group of twenty insurgents took over the wing of the mall that has the most high-end shops as well as a small bank branch. Their position has allowed them to have a large sum of money within their reach. And now, with hostages, the leader of the group is working to gather an even bigger ransom.

"SWAT arrived and is slowly emptying wings and stores, looking for anyone who needs assistance. Police started negotiations, and the FBI is en route to take over. These guys are trained and ready for action."

Danica worked the bill of her hat lower over her face. "So, what's their play? How are they going to get out? This place was locked down fast, and thanks to Evan, they've already lost some men."

Buck nodded. "Danica, you and Sergio get to work and see

what the possibilities are for a safe exit. I was informed Homeland has an interest and is looking into the identities of the deceased from the bookstore."

Sergio tugged Danica's arm as they headed for the van, pausing halfway.

"Uh, Evan, you wanna handle this?" She grinned.

"Yeah, give me a sec," Evan muttered as he pushed past her with a grunt.

4

Bexley's head went up as her mind suddenly engaged.
Grimacing, she pulled the side of her shirt up and noticed the angry purple and black bruising working its way across her side. Her whole body ached from being pulled around by her hair.

Taking slow, steady breaths, she focused on the small compartment with a fold-out desk on either side, computers lining the space. If this was the command center, as the van's side stated, where were all the people from Navy's unit? Evan, that was his name, Evan something ...

Her eyelids closed again as she leaned her head back, shifting her body and gripping her side. Evan had wanted to help, and she should've let him. She groaned as their conversation pushed through her mind.

Pulling that man from the door had seemed like a good idea at the time. She thought it would help seal the room, maybe even help ID their attacker. But Evan wouldn't understand. He would have no idea her experience, her abilities in that kind of situation.

"Lord, You've got to help me out here," she mumbled with a wince.

The realization hit that she no longer had any self-confidence, much less control over her anger. How did she get here?

Pushing herself to stand, she groaned and took a few steps, hoping movement would ease the muscle spasms working their way through her neck. She had just got to the door when it swung open.

Readying herself for another verbal spar, she backed up as Evan stepped inside.

"Have a seat, Bexley," he mumbled.

His large frame made the small space seem cramped as he found his chair again and tossed his hat on the counter, freeing a mass of short blond hair. He ran his fingers back and forth across the top. She sat with a grimace, spinning so that she wasn't facing him.

"How're you feeling?" he asked softly.

She narrowed her eyes at this new development.

"What? I'm just asking."

"Fine, I'm fine," she mumbled.

"You don't act fine."

She kept her gaze forward as the sounds of drawers opening echoed in the silence.

"Here, drink." He set a cold bottle of water next to her and she pushed her right hand into it, letting the coolness work into her aching joints.

"Sorry, I should've got you some ice."

"It's fine," she mumbled.

Working to open the bottle, she took a few drinks before holding it against her hand once again.

"Let me see."

He scooted the chair into her space and she flinched, pushing back to create some distance.

"Easy. I'm just trying to help." His eyebrows furrowed as he watched her for a moment, then dropped his gaze.

He held her hand steady, fingers moving over her knuckles. His hands were huge compared to hers. They became gentle as he moved her fingers and rubbed his thumb across the bloody knuckles, making her wince.

"Probably have some breaks in there."

"It's fine," she whispered.

"Let me see your side."

He started to reach across when she jerked his hand away, bending back his thumb. His reaction trumped hers as he bent back her left hand, and a small cry escaped her lips.

"Sorry, I'm sorry. It's reaction." He held her hand once again, sighing heavily. "Sorry. Really, I ..."

"It's fine."

"You say that a lot."

She looked up. The intensity of his stare didn't match his gentle, concerned tone. Suddenly uncomfortable, she pulled at her hand, but he refused to let go, holding it with both of his. She started to look away again when he shifted to get into her vision.

"I ..."

"Just wait," he sighed as he looked inclined to speak, but words never came.

A loud bang on the door made her jump as his head turned.

"Come on, I've got to get you elsewhere so we can use the van," he mumbled.

She pulled her injured hand back into her body. "Why can't I go home?"

"You're a witness and need to be interviewed."

"There are probably a hundred officers standing around. I'm sure one of them can do it."

He stood, stooped over to keep from hitting his head. "*We* have to interview you."

She shrugged. "Fine, send in one of your friends."

"We're a little busy right now."

"It doesn't look like it to me." Her voice dropped as she realized she was just pushing his buttons again, arguing for some strange reason with the man who had saved her life.

He groaned and held his hand out. "Let's go."

Grimacing, she pushed herself up to stand, and he took hold of her elbow.

"Don't." She yanked away.

"Just trying to help." His voice was controlled, calm.

"I don't want you to," she whispered, her eyes dropping from his. Pulling the water bottle to her chest, she crinkled the plastic.

He sighed and pushed his hat on his head as he went before her to the steps. Taking a breath, she slowly made it down as he held the door, this time refusing to put out a hand to help.

"This way." His hand found her back again as she tried to move away. The more she strayed, the more he pulled her back to him.

"Back off, Evan." She looked up at the sound of his chuckle. "What?"

"You finally used my name." He glanced down, and she hated to see that grin on his face.

Good grief, what was wrong with her? A handsome man had saved her from a hostage situation, and she was frustrated that he smiled at her? She really was messed up.

Peering over her shoulder, she noted one of the men who had come to help earlier was following as they crossed the parking lot.

Evan pulled at her waist again. Quickly shoving his hand off her side, she followed, crossing her free hand over her stomach as if willing her body to remain intact. The way she felt right now, she might not make it home in one piece.

Stopping at an SUV, he pulled open the back door and she slowly climbed in, groaning from bending over as she collapsed in the seat. Evan pushed in behind her, and she frowned as she scooted over for him to sit.

Fighter

"Why am I sitting here?"

He pulled a clipboard out. "Okay, I need your phone number and address."

She sighed and answered his questions one by one.

"Emergency contact?"

She opened her mouth for a moment and then closed it, leaning forward on her knees.

"Um, just put Reggie White."

"Relationship?"

"Friend." She rattled off her cell phone number and sat back in the seat, holding the bottle against her hand once again.

"No family?"

She shook her head.

He bumped her leg with his. "Hey, you okay?"

"Yeah, fine." She cleared her throat as she gazed out the side window.

He sighed again, and she heard him pushing papers around. "Okay, they've started negotiations, so we don't know when we'll be going in. SWAT has it covered, and we're on standby. After that, we'll finish the interview."

"Sure."

"There's some more water in that cooler if you need some." He nodded to the blue cooler at her feet. "Remember, don't leave, and I'll be back when this is all over to get an official statement of what happened."

She nodded again.

"You need some ice or someone to take a look at your side?"

Shaking her head, the let-down of adrenaline and the emotions that came with it flooded her. She wanted him to leave, right now, before she fell apart in front of him.

"Bexley?"

"Can you just go?" She cleared her throat, biting the inside of her cheek to hold in her tears as she looked away.

"If you need something, let one of the officers know."

She nodded and heard another sigh as the door pulled open

and then slammed closed. Balling up on her good side, unwanted tears flooded her vision, the weariness of the situation weighing on top of her as her body ached and burned.

5

Pacing outside the command center, Evan glanced at the SUV where Bexley waited before turning to head back the other direction. His mind spun as he relived holding her hand and feeling very much on edge.

She was the strongest woman he had ever met, tough and ornery, and ... beautiful. Her rust-colored hair hung mostly in her face, long curls falling over her shoulders, and she had the brightest green eyes he'd ever seen.

She had played a surprisingly good grief-stricken hostage. He almost saw tears in her eyes. He couldn't contain his smile at her gripping his shirt, leaning into him and letting him hold her tightly to get to her gun.

Pretty? Yes. Stubborn, argumentative, tough, he could think of a few other adjectives to describe her, but they were definitely not on the list he was trying to use to deter his focus.

Shaking his head, he stifled a chuckle. To think he went to the mall today to get a new Bible. Instead, he followed a pretty woman through the bookstore and ended up helping save a room full of people.

Man, God sure had a sense of humor.

He continued pacing, blowing out a breath as his nerves

itched. Usually, he found an easy way out of attraction, especially when that someone was part of a hostage take over that he was working.

His mind compartmentalized things easily. If it didn't fit or had problems, then it needed to be dropped. His attraction to her could easily be a problem, but he couldn't seem to drop it.

"What's on your mind, Ev?"

He frowned at Haiden. Coming to a stop in front of his ever-silent teammate, Evan glared. "I think there's something on yours."

Narrowing his gaze, Haiden only kept his perfect posture, arms crossed over his rifle. Haiden was the typical sniper—calm, precise, and without distraction.

"You seem vexed. Y'know ... women can do that to you. It's a known fact." Haiden's slow drawl pushed out the words.

"I don't get vexed."

Haiden let a chuckle escape. "Sorry, it slipped out."

"What's taking so long?" Evan grunted as he continued his pacing.

Buck and Jeff were busy with the negotiator, helping to ease the tension of the situation. He hoped they had a good plan because, based on the way those men worked and moved, they were well trained. That didn't bode well for the hostages. Danica and Sergio were working on the building's blueprints to find an escape route. There had to be more to the story than what they were seeing.

"Okay, I think we've got it." Sergio pulled the door open and motioned for them to come inside.

Ducking his head once again, he climbed up into the van and found space to kneel next to the computer where Danica sat. Hat off, she had her jet black hair pulled up in a ponytail.

Evan leaned in to view her computer screen.

"There's a tunnel underneath that wing of the mall that runs to the east." Danica pointed to the abandoned system just feet from the basement wall of what appeared to be the bookstore.

"If they brought equipment to dig, they might be planning to tunnel into the inactive system and sneak away unnoticed."

"Based on the video feed I received from the mall, they have all sorts of equipment. Large duffle bags and rolling cases," Sergio muttered as he stared at Danica's screen.

Evan frowned. "What tunnel? What's it from?"

"Looks like remnants from the Santa Fe station. The underground railroad system that moved products from the train station up to the shopping district back in the twenties."

"And the mall is close enough to tunnel through?"

Danica shrugged at Haiden's question. "Yeah, if they don't collapse the tunnel wall by digging. The structure has been hidden underground and abandoned for so long I doubt there's much left that's stable."

"No explosives then?" Evan asked.

"It's possible, but dangerous."

"Then they're taking a huge risk."

Evan glanced at Haiden and nodded his agreement. "Where do the tunnels lead?"

"Most end back at the railway station, but according to some of my research, there's a line that supposedly moves all the way to Santa Fe, New Mexico."

"Then that's the one they'll take. They have to know that the train station would be one of the first places we'd lock down. It's the closest way out," Sergio muttered.

Evan nodded. "Push the info through to Buck, see what he says. It might be the break we need should they make their way out." He started to stand as Sergio jumped out, but Danica caught his attention.

"Got some info on your girl."

"Who?"

"Bexley Bowers?"

"Oh, yeah? What'd you find?"

Now she had his attention.

"Bexley's job history puts her as a licensed specialized

protection agent for Litigation Press, a group of lawyers who apparently need round-the-clock protection. She's been a bodyguard since 2013. Two months ago, that changed. Now she has a part-time job at the public library."

He smirked, trying to cover his amusement at the woman he had just met being a librarian. "Well, that explains her insight into getting the body out of the door and her hand-to-hand skills."

"That's what I thought too. I did find some more personal background. But it's not good."

"What happened?"

Danica frowned. "Her family was killed in a plane crash."

"Her family? Like, all of them?"

"Yeah, her parents, an aunt, uncle, and brother. She has only a few relatives left, none of them live around here."

Nausea rolled through his stomach. Dropping his hat to the ground, he rubbed his hand back and forth over his head.

"She seems pretty competent, wonder if I should bring it up with Buck?"

He sighed. "Bring what up?"

"We're one short and could use some more help. I, for one, would like to have another woman involved. You guys are a pain."

He stared at her grin, his irritation building. "I don't think that's a good idea," he muttered.

"Why? She seems pretty talented, maybe even interested in learning a new career?" Danica grinned with a wink.

He grumbled, shoved his hat on his head, and stepped outside. Slamming the door to the vehicle, he went back to his pacing, annoyed that Danica would even consider talking to Buck about bringing on someone as green as Bexley.

They all had their backgrounds—military or police—education, and experience that made them the choice for these kinds of situations. But even working as a bodyguard for any period of time was nothing compared to what they handled.

Fighter

This detail was about providing backup to hostage situations, backing up other agencies dealing with heavily armed attackers and how to break them down, not just protect against them.

He glanced at the SUV Bexley sat in, shaking his head as he spun to see Danica exiting the command van.

"So, you do a lot of homework?"

Although former ATF, Danica had a knack for computers. So what had she found on him?

She shrugged. "Yeah? So?"

"Do you dig like that on all of us too?" He narrowed his eyes as her jaw dropped.

She stepped into his space, obviously not concerned at her small stature next to his. She glared up at him. "I don't do that to team members. If there's something we need to know, I assume you will say something, or Buck will. Bexley's trained in some manner and appeared to conduct herself well today. But if you're that put out about it, I won't mention it."

"Thanks." He shook his head as he walked away, his mind still spinning about Bexley and her past.

Now more than ever he wanted to find a way to offer some comfort. She already had experienced too much trauma in her life to be sitting in that SUV and dealing with this all alone.

"Let's go." Buck's hollow voice sounded above the noise of the parking lot filled with police. "Things aren't going well. Between the FBI's negotiator and then Jeff, whoever it is isn't backing down. We're going to have to breach."

"With hostages?" Evan shook his head. "You said there were, what, sixty people in there?"

Buck nodded. "Sniper says before the blinds were drawn in the bank, he saw at least that many, their hands being zip-tied and pushed to the floor."

"We're taking a chance," Haiden mumbled.

"I agree." Buck let out a breath. "Go get Danica and Sergio. We're going to need all the help we can get."

6

"Finish your job!"

Shouting at the hired men around him, he paced, waiting for the explosion that would gain him access to his prize.

A round man in tactical gear made his way in front of them. "We've got no out. The police, FBI, everyone's here, and the whole place is surrounded."

"I want that safe. Now," he shouted.

The other men pulled their rifles around as one worked on the detonator.

"We lost too much time in the bookstore. Once I detonate, we won't have time to breach. What we did get out will have to be enough."

He glared at the inept men he had hired to complete this mission. The sixty or so hostages began to talk, their voices rising as his men yelled at them to quiet down. It was time. There was nothing more they could do here. His mission would have to wait.

Anger flooded his senses. Seizing a female hostage, he ignored the woman's cries. "I've got an out. You should've thought ahead," he sneered. "I want this place to burn down.

Take what you've got and blow it. At least I won't have to finish paying you for your incompetence."

Raising the gun to her head, he waited for the distraction that would lead him out of here and this mess. "Idiots," he murmured as he gripped the woman's throat in the crook of his arm.

The cache would have to wait, but it would be his soon.

BEXLEY SAT STRAIGHT UP at the sound of the crash, the rumble of the ground shaking the van. A huge cloud of dust covered the area where the mall once sat. Officers and medical personnel rushed toward the building as the dust started to settle, revealing a gaping hole in the mall's outer wall.

Pushing open the door, everyone converged on what was left of the building's outer wall. Police assisted several men and women from the hole in the wall, all had their hands bound behind their backs. Bexley hobbled toward the command center van, shouts echoing as officers directed the hostages.

A scream from her right made her step around the van. Clothed in body armor, a man walked backward from the gaping hole. She immediately recognized her smelly attacker, holding a hostage as a shield and backing away to the parking lot.

Her breath caught in her throat. The woman he held was crying out as the assailant drug her by the neck.

Climbing into the back of the van, she dug through the drawers, hoping for a weapon but coming up empty. A familiar case sat in the drawer and she pulled it out. One earwig remained. She pushed it into her ear and heard muted voices.

Stepping from the van and around the side, Bexley narrowed her eyes at the debris still in the air. Her attacker hid behind his hostage, holding her steady. Bexley knew having a human shield would make it a tough shot, even for a sniper. Hitting the

Fighter

assailant and not the woman he held captive wasn't impossible, but it would be difficult.

Evan and his team edged toward the duo. From her hiding spot, Bexley could hear a man trying to negotiate without luck.

"Get back or she dies," her attacker shouted.

"Easy. We're here to help you get out of this."

"Who says I need out of this?"

Bexley's heart raced as she realized her attacker would easily kill the woman, even if it meant he would die.

She took off toward the SUV, muffled voices still sounding in her ear, nothing positive about the situation or the assailant.

"No, he's not backing down."

"We need an alternate exit for him before he shoots the hostage."

"Get him steady. He's moving too much."

Climbing into the driver's seat, she found the keys and drove the SUV where she could watch. The plan forming in her mind wasn't foolproof, but sitting here doing nothing wasn't an option either. She parked out of the line of fire.

"No more talking. She dies!"

"No shot, I've got no shot." One of the voices from earlier sounded clearly through the earwig.

"God, this might not be the best idea," she muttered. She drove toward the man, pausing where he could see her as she slid from the seat. "Take it and go," she shouted from behind the door.

Heat flushed her face as she felt all eyes on her.

"Come on." Her attacker dragged the woman toward the vehicle.

"Wait, let her go first," Bexley shouted.

"Nice try, she stays with me."

Gritting her teeth, she advanced on the man. He took notice and raised his arm.

"Stop, or she dies!"

Bexley paused, noting a small bump in the woman's lower abdomen through her snug shirt. Bexley's stomach dropped.

"No ... No, take me." Bexley put her hands up and made her way toward the two.

"Bexley," Evan shouted as she took hold of the woman's hand.

"Take me, leave her."

The man's dark eyes were wide as he glanced from her to the team. "Fine, I owe you anyway."

She stepped in front of the woman, searching the team until she saw Evan's face. His hat gone, his steely eyes glared as he pumped his gun up and then down. The man's arm gripped her neck, and she stood solid.

"Move," he snarled.

"Not until she's safe," she stammered.

The woman crawled and then stood as a few men in tactical gear grabbed her up, pulling her away.

"What's she doing?"

The voice echoed in her head and she forced a smile, finding Evan's eyes once again. The grip around her neck tightened, and she grabbed at his arm, taking advantage of the movement to turn her head and tap her ear surreptitiously.

"Now, move." His hot breath made her want to gag as she side-stepped to the driver's side.

"Bex!" Evan's voice came through again as she felt the barrel of the gun push into her temple.

7

Evan unloaded his clip, attempting to flatten the SUV's tire before they could leave. But since it was property of TRT, the tires would stay drivable for several miles before the vehicle would be compromised.

"Mitchell. Holster that weapon," Buck's shouts rang out, but Evan couldn't stop.

As the trigger gave him an empty click, he lowered his weapon, breathing heavily.

"What ... what just happened?" Evan grunted as he leaned over at the waist.

"She had a reason. Let's see if we can figure out what." Danica's voice sounded from behind.

"Evan, a word."

He shoved his weapon in its holster and waited for Buck to reprimand him.

"Why were you firing on a vehicle where a hostage is present?"

"I was trying to disable the vehicle, keep it here."

Buck's eyes narrowed. "With a hostage inside?"

Evan took a deep breath. "I'm a good shot, sir. I wasn't putting anyone in danger."

Buck pushed into his space, squaring off with him. Evan waited for a tongue lashing. Buck was as tall as him but lanky. He crossed his long arms and glared.

"I understand your intent. But those aren't the rules, and you know it." Buck took a breath. "Look, I wanted you on this team. You belong on this team. But you have to play by the rules just like we do. I don't do off-book, Lieutenant."

Evan clenched his jaw and nodded.

"Now, what made her do that?"

"I ... I don't have any idea." Evan shook his head.

"Then let's see what Danica can figure out."

Evan nodded with a sigh and followed Buck to the command center.

"Take a look at this." Danica pulled up footage from the van and rewound the video feed that she had left up and running.

The footage showed Bexley coming in and sifting through the drawers and then pulling out a box. She slipped something small into her ear.

"So, she could hear us?" Haiden asked as he collapsed in a chair.

"Looks like it." Evan huffed and ran his hands back and forth through his hair. "She smiled and winked at one point. She must've heard you say there wasn't a shot and decided to find another way to free the hostage." He held his hand to his chin. "With that earwig, can we track her?"

"Not likely." Sergio shrugged. "Bluetooth gives us a signal, but it's not strong enough to track."

"What about the nav system in the car?" Haiden's drawl echoed.

"That we can do, if he hasn't disabled it." Sergio started typing on his computer.

Evan looked over to Buck.

"Let's go." Buck nodded.

Evan jumped from the van with Haiden at his side, then rushed to his SUV. The command center van started up and they followed close behind. His hands gripped the wheel as his heart pounded in his ears.

"You okay?"

They hadn't even been on the road for five minutes before Haiden spoke. He was usually the quiet one.

"Just great." Evan huffed. "The woman I rescued ended up sacrificing herself to a lunatic, the same one she clocked before this whole thing started. He'll take her out the second he gets a chance," he muttered.

"Don't let it get to you."

Evan stared at Haiden a moment before putting his eyes back on the road. "I'll be fine." He shook his head. "What made her do that anyway?"

"She's a woman, Ev. Don't try and figure it out."

Danica's voice came over the radio. "Okay, finally found the signal. We're a few miles out. With traffic, things might get hairy."

Evan huffed. "Keep at it. Have Sergio pull up some alternate maps, maybe we can catch up faster."

"On it."

His jaw clenched as he white-knuckled the steering wheel. The urgency of the situation pushed into him as bile churned in his gut.

Why did she do that? Why did Bexley take that woman's place?

BEXLEY'S SIDE burned like fire, and she swallowed the bile filling her throat. Her captor shoved a gun into her side as he drove. "You'll never make it out. They know what you look like. I bet they already have your name," she gritted between her teeth.

"Shut up."

A blow to the side of her head dazed her a moment, flashes of light filling her vision. Holding her forehead, she tried to inhale but the pain in her side was too great, her body crumpled into the door.

"I'm tired of waiting, and now it's gone." His voice sounded far away as she closed her eyes. The world blurred. Gradually, she became aware of a new pain.

Straining against the pull on her hair, her eyes popped open to find the SUV parked inside a building, the passenger door open.

She hit the cement floor and collapsed.

"Walk," he sneered.

Pushing herself up, she hobbled farther inside what looked like a warehouse, self-defense moves running through her mind. But with her hand injury and the dizziness still hanging on, she knew it was pointless. There was no way she could pack a punch that would help her escape.

He shoved her into a chair and then used zip ties to secure a wrist to each side behind her back. Her ankles were zip-tied even tighter to the legs of the metal chair.

"See if you can work your way out of that."

His breath made her look away, attempting to find some kind of escape from the smell.

"Why? Why are you doing this?" Her breathing was labored, and dizziness forced her eyes shut.

"I have my reasons. Now, quiet. You talk, I'll shut you up." His fingers held her face, gripping her chin tightly before he shoved her head to the side.

Her shoulders burned from being secured so far behind her body, and she worked to relax the muscles. Forcing her eyes open, she took in her surroundings just in case the earwig started working again. At the moment, nothing but static echoed in her ear from the device.

The only things in her vision were old machines and rusted barrels. It looked like a machine shop or a recycling center, perhaps. Light barely filtered through the window as the smell of oil and diesel filled her senses.

She turned her head, but with her upper body trapped by the zip ties on her wrists and the aching muscles in her neck, she couldn't see where he went.

"There's no way I can get it now. Either you send me men that will do what I ask or prepare yourself. I won't allow another failure."

Bexley managed to squeak out, "What were you looking for? I can help."

Maybe if she could help him, it would give her a chance to survive.

"Shut up!" He suddenly appeared in front of her, a sneer on his lips. "You can't help me. You've ruined everything."

He disappeared once more.

After what felt like a lifetime of bangs, clicks, and cursing, her assailant appeared again, shoving something under both of her legs and then settling behind her. His proximity made her breathing pick up as she tried to keep her head down, her hair covering the earpiece. She had thought it clever to put it in, but now the static it transmitted only made her head pound even more.

"You have a bomb set up beneath you." His chuckle pained her stomach. "You move, it goes off, you try and break the chair, it goes off."

"What? Why are you doing this?" Bile rose in her throat, burning as she tried to swallow.

"You have twenty minutes." He stood in front of her, a large duffle bag over his shoulder. "I'm just paying you back for the loss of my team. Your breach was my downfall." He grimaced before turning and disappearing from her line of vision. "Enjoy your last moments on earth."

8

"Bexley?"

The muffled voice echoed as Bexley struggled to wake. Prying her eyes open, she closed them again as her head pounded in her ears.

"Bexley?"

Where was the voice coming from?

"Bex? You alone?"

Evan. It was Evan's voice.

"I ... I think so, but ... but there's a bomb under my chair, you need to leave." Her gruff voice made her throat burn.

She took a breath as her head hung down, the muscles in her neck pulling and straining. No one spoke. The muffled tap of rubber boots on the concrete floor got louder, then stopped.

"What can you tell me about the bomb?"

Evan's voice was calm and collected, just like when the assailants detained everyone in the back room. She heard him moving closer and lower, probably stooping behind her chair, and struggled to get out a warning.

"He said if I move, it will go off. He slid something under my legs. Then he said I had twenty minutes." Her raspy voice raw from tears. "I don't know how long it's been, but it has to be close to twenty. You need to leave."

"Don't move."

"What do you see?" Another male voice cut into the com in her ear.

"C-4, motion trigger, and a dummy trigger. The connection under her leg is interesting. I'm not sure if it's real."

"You better be sure, Ev. Time?" The same male voice from earlier sounded.

"Three minutes," Evan mumbled.

"Get out. All of you, please." She did what she could to strengthen her voice, but she had a hard time getting any sound to come out.

A deep breath sounded.

"Here we go. Haiden, take a walk."

"No, man. I'm good." Haiden's voice came out strong from farther behind her.

She blew out a breath, knowing Evan was working on a device that could easily kill all of them.

God, please spare them.

9

"We're good."

Evan heard everyone breathe a sigh in his ear as he pulled the wires away from the bomb. Stepping in front of Bexley, he knelt and clipped the zip ties on her ankles and wrists.

"Okay, come on, Bex." He motioned Haiden out. "Go make sure the ambulance is ready."

Haiden nodded, turning to leave the building.

"Bexley, I'll help you stand, come on."

Her shoulders slumped as she held her arm to her chest. She was done. The amazing fighter in the mall finally succumbed to the fear and pain she had fought all day.

He gently pulled her right hand away, noticing the swelling and the blood around her wrist from the ties. Taking a deep breath, he exhaled angrily.

Pulling out his ear com, he gently pushed under her hair to find her ear com and pocketed both.

"Bex, look at me." He lifted her chin as his stomach dropped.

Her eyes were red and glassy, blood pooled on the side of her face where her attacker had obviously hit, making a large, purple bruise. Her lips were cracked, and he wanted nothing more than to pull her into his arms and carry her out of here.

"I'm going to help you up, okay?"

The fire gone from her eyes, they dropped from his as she nodded. Taking her elbows, he helped her stand, her shaky legs barely holding as she groaned and grasped her side. This time, when he pulled her hand away and lifted her shirt slightly, she didn't try to stop him. The skin was deep purple, turning dark blue and black across her entire side.

"Bex, I'm so sorry," he mumbled and stepped closer, wanting to hug her, comfort her.

She took a deep breath, her body stiffening. "I ... I'm fine." Her voice was barely audible.

His stomach clenched as her sudden change made him nauseous. Even injured and barely responsive, she was unsure of him.

Why would she react like that?

"Hey, Ev. FBI wants to clear it."

He nodded at Jeff's voice.

"We need to get to the ambulance," he mumbled.

He turned, his hand barely brushing her elbow, and she took a step with a groan.

"I'm going to carry you. I don't think you can walk. Okay?"

She simply nodded and all but collapsed in his arms as he pulled her to him, her injured side facing outward. Holding her close, she rolled into his chest, gripping his vest and mumbling something.

"Bex? What'd you say?" He looked down, her eyes closed and her body went limp. He frowned as he carried her out, worried he was hurting her further as she lay passed out in his arms.

Gently setting her on the gurney, the EMTs did a check and started an IV before they got her loaded.

"Where're you headed?" Evan asked as the EMT slammed the doors shut.

"Northwest General."

He watched as the ambulance left, a weight suddenly heavy on his shoulders.

Haiden came up beside him. "She okay?"

"She's taken a beating. I guess we'll find out soon enough. And next time I say to take a walk, you might want to do so."

"Nah, I trust you'll take care of it." Haiden shrugged, then headed for the van.

BEXLEY GROANED. Where was she?

There was a soft pillow and bed beneath her. She pulled at the scratchy blanket over her arms. Her burning throat ached, but she heard no one around to speak to, anyway. Straining against the light in the room, she forced her eyes open as she searched the bed for the call button.

"Can I help you?" The loud sound of the voice through the speaker made her grimace.

"I need to see a nurse or the doctor, please." She cleared her throat painfully.

"He's on his way."

Punching the buttons on the side of the bed, she finally found the one to raise her head as her vision cleared. Holding her right hand up, she noticed the brace that fit from her fingers to just past her wrist. Hurting and feeling more than a little lost, all she wanted to do now was go home.

After an uneventful discussion with her doctor about her injuries, the nurse handed her a cup of ice.

"Just take it slow." She coiled the IV line around the pole.

"Can I leave?" Bexley whispered.

"I'll talk to the doctor and see if we can get the paperwork started." The nurse leaned over Bexley's head. "You'll need to take care of those stitches."

"I will."

As the nurse left, two men walked in.

"Miss Bowers? My name is Detective Mills. I need to speak to you about what happened."

"I'll tell you what I can, but I don't know much," she whispered, her eyes darting to the man in the suit behind Detective Mills.

"This is Agent Falls."

"Ma'am."

She returned the agent's nod.

"Just start from the beginning, when you first encountered the situation, and go from there."

After sucking on some ice chips and answering some questions, her throat eased. She went through the day, relating information from the mall and then to the hostage situation she intruded upon and the bomb.

"Thanks for your input. You were very brave."

"More like stupid," she muttered as she tried to sit up in the bed.

"If you need anything or have any questions, please don't hesitate to call."

She nodded, taking the offered card.

The nurse returned with a packet of information on how to take care of her stitches.

"If you have any issues, call your primary physician. And keep the movement to a minimum."

"Of course. Thanks."

"Here's some scrubs. Those detectives took everything with them."

"Oh, okay," she mumbled, accepting the offered clothes.

"You want some help?"

"No, I'm good." Offering a smile, Bexley nodded to the nurse.

Dressing as quickly as she could in the bathroom, she refrained from looking in the mirror. The stinging pain and the feeling of swelling indicated how bad her face would look. Her side strained as she tried to pull back her hair.

"Forget it," she muttered as she used a washcloth to wipe

down her aching face and ignored the tangled mess that fell about her shoulders.

Sliding on the hospital slippers, she paused. Her purse, phone, and keys were still at the mall. With a groan, she made her way back to the room and sat on the bed. How was she going to get home when she had no way to pay for a ride?

She did have a spare key hidden in her backyard, but she figured the cab driver wouldn't appreciate not getting paid as she left the cab and went to the back of her home to get the extra key. And Reggie, well, she mentioned being busy with work and could easily be out of town by now.

"Good grief," she muttered as she slid from the bed and made her way to the window, wavering with each step.

Hospital lights lit up the parking lot below the window while an orange-and red-tinted sky loomed in the background. She tried to take a breath and groaned at the pain ripping through her side.

She closed her eyes and leaned her forehead to the cool glass.

God had given her a second chance today. That bomb was set to go off, and if Evan and his team hadn't shown up ...

The past two months had become a nightmare and tonight sealed her former life. The loss of her family and diving into a life of meaningless relationships had to end. Then there was Tennison, her last boyfriend and the man she had fallen for—hard.

But his anger and all the fighting led her to breakup with him, which led to the loss of her job. That job had been her anchor, giving her life meaning, and she'd given it all up for him. Now, she was determined to find God's will, and that started with a new beginning.

The door opened behind her, and she held her hand up. "I know, I'm leaving."

"How do you plan to do that?"

Evan's voice hung in the air. She froze for a moment before turning slowly. He stood at the bed, setting down her purse before facing her. Clad in jeans and a T-shirt, he pulled off his hat and stuck the bill in a back pocket.

"You didn't answer my question."

"I—I can call a cab. Thanks for bringing my things." She started to say something else but couldn't find the words.

"I'll drive you. Let's go." He nodded toward the door, waiting, as if he knew she wouldn't agree.

"You don't have to go out of your way. Thanks for my purse. I'm calling a cab."

"Bexley, do you see me here asking? How is it going out of my way?"

Exhaustion washed over her as she looked away, slowly walking to her purse and feeling very self-conscious. How rough did she look? She knew her hair was a mess and her face hurt badly enough she had to have a bruise.

Fiddling with the purse, she found her phone inside, fully charged, and all her things, including her keys.

"My car. Is my car still at the mall?"

"I don't know, the mall's a crime scene. You'll have to leave it."

She nodded. "And my gun?"

Swallowing took effort, and she closed her eyes and gripped her throat as the burning ached.

"Not yet, but I'll make sure you get it back." His soft voice soothed her much more than she wanted to admit. "I'll get you a wheelchair."

"I ... I don't need one." Protocol or not, she wasn't being wheeled out with Evan here.

Shouldering the purse, she made herself look at him, those steely blue eyes staring.

"Come on then." He stepped away from the bed and waited for her to go in front.

She worked to smooth down her hair, tucking it behind her ears and grimacing at every motion.

"How bad?"

"I have to take it easy, but nothing's broken," she muttered as she hobbled down the hall and into the elevator. "I just want to go home."

Tears threatened, and she held them back. How could she even have any tears left after today?

He refrained from leading her as they made it through the hallways and the elevator, keeping his hands to himself as they walked slowly through the parking lot. She found the pace both frustrating and necessary.

Evan had rescued her three times now, twice from danger and now from the hospital. Already finding him extremely attractive, the last thing she needed was him pushing the bounds of ... well, whatever this was.

There was no way she could jump into a physical relationship where she would fall right back into her old ways.

He paused at a large truck and opened the passenger door. Gripping the door handle and stepping up, she groaned as she pulled herself into the seat.

"You good?" He stood in the door frame, his jaw tense.

Looking away, she nodded, then jumped as he slammed the door shut.

He started the car and headed out of the lot, obviously sure where she lived. How? Ah, paperwork—they filled out paperwork earlier, including her address.

The drive continued in silence as she leaned her head back and sank into the seat, closing her eyes and feeling herself fall away.

10

When they arrived at Bexley's house, she was still asleep, her body rolled toward the door.

After easing the passenger door open, Evan stepped into the space.

"Bex?" he said gently.

She jumped and then muffled a yell as she gripped her side, slumping forward in the seat.

"Sorry, I didn't know how else to wake you up." He held out a hand. "Let me help you down, okay?"

She only nodded again as she swung her legs around. Taking her right and left elbows, he pulled her to him and down without pushing into her side. Her left hand gripped his arm tightly as she took a few breaths.

"Bexley?"

"I'm good, thanks," she whispered, her body still shaking.

He pulled her purse out and shut the door before taking her arm, aiding her walk to the bungalow. As she reached for her purse, he dug out the keys. Without a word, he opened the door and helped her inside.

She seemed almost in a daze as she walked inside, kicking off her shoes and taking the purse from him as she dug out her phone. He watched her put in her alarm code twice, her brows furrowing.

"Bexley, can you call someone? I'm not sure you should be here alone."

Between the pain and being taken hostage—twice—she looked out of it. Considering the stitches, she could easily have a concussion.

"No, no one." She shook her head and closed her eyes as she leaned against the wall.

He stepped in front, refraining from helping to steady her, but barely.

"I ... I need to lie down," she mumbled.

As she opened her eyes, he saw the glassy look and realized she probably had a dose of pain medicine before she was discharged.

"Did they give you some medicine?"

"Yeah, I have a prescription too, somewhere ..." she trailed off, brows knitted together.

Her hand gripped his, and he paused for a moment as she started down the hallway with him in tow. His heart jumped. Walking around in this woman's home, to her bedroom, was not where he pictured this going. Not that anything could happen, would happen.

Collapsing on her bed, she released his hand as she set her phone down on the table. "Why ... why're you here?"

She eased under the blankets with a groan. Helping to pull the blankets over her, he sat down.

"I was worried about you. You've had a bad day."

She leaned back against the headboard for a moment, closing her eyes.

"I'm going to turn on the alarm after I leave, okay? I put my number in your phone, call me if you need something." He tapped her wrist until she opened her eyes.

"Oh, I ... I guess I'm just a little confused. I, the medicine they gave me ..." she trailed off again, holding her head. "My head really hurts," she whispered.

"You need to give yourself some time to process."

Her eyes went wide as she looked up at him. "He ... Did you get that guy?"

He frowned at the fear on her face. "No, but we've seen his face, and everyone is looking for him."

Her gaze dropped to the bed. He held his hands together in front of him as he leaned in on his knees. "Bex, you're safe here. There's no reason he would know who you are or how to find you, okay?"

She nodded as she took a breath and closed her eyes again. It killed him to keep his hands to himself, not taking her hands or wrapping his arms around her to give her some comfort.

When her eyes opened, he noticed something different, a little bit of that fire returning.

"Thanks for driving me. I'm good. I'll set the alarm." She pulled the blankets back as he held his hand up to stop her.

"I can set it. I saw your code. Just get some rest."

She started to talk and he leaned in. "Rest. I imagine this was probably the worst day of your life, but—"

"Not even close." Her scratchy voice came out terse as she stared.

He nodded, remembering the information about her family. "I'm leaving. Get some rest. My number is in your phone."

"I won't need it, but thanks." She tacked on the last part, but he could tell she didn't want to.

He nodded. "Take care, Bexley. Just to let you know, my boss will call you tomorrow."

"Why would he want to talk to me?"

He shrugged. "Just to get the report in your own words."

"I spoke to the detective in charge—"

"Yeah, but not us." He forced himself to stand, shoving his hands in his pockets to keep from reaching out or doing something else stupid. "See you later."

He turned, blowing out a long breath and fast walking to the door before he changed his mind. He set the alarm, then hustled to the truck and shoved himself inside with a grunt.

"Easy man, this is not the situation you need to be in," he muttered.

He chastised himself for wanting to stay, wanting to help her in any way he could. But she had some skeletons in her closet. Although she seemed just fine letting him guide her inside her home, the way she backed away from him in the van earlier, practically defending herself, didn't fit.

Driving to the office, Evan worked to keep his emotions in check.

Where had this come from?

"God, seriously? You can't do this to me. I'm not that guy, remember?"

He had already had this talk with God long ago. All was good until about three years ago.

After signing up for the Navy straight out of high school, he knew he wasn't boyfriend material. He had dated, but nothing substantial or long-term. He wasn't made for that. His brain just didn't do relationships. The drama, the neediness, it wasn't something he wanted to deal with.

He'd thought God agreed.

So far, he had never met any woman that kept his attention. Attraction, yeah, but he was always upfront about what he wanted, and a relationship wasn't it.

But with Bexley—there was something about her, something that pulled at him, and he wanted very badly to give in. If they had just caught her kidnapper, Evan could walk away with nothing but a little attraction lingering. But right now, knowing her captor was loose, he had much more than a little attraction weighing on him.

"Just give it time. They'll catch the guy, and all this will pass," he muttered.

The day took its toll on Evan, especially after seeing Bexley trade places with that woman by choice. Who does that? Who sacrifices themselves for someone they don't even know?

Swallowing hard, he pulled into the TRT parking lot and sat for a minute, working to ease the clenching in his chest. He needed to keep his focus.

"Not now, God. I really can't do this now."

After finally getting back into a career, losing everything, and starting over, he needed to keep his focus. And Bexley Bowers couldn't be his focus.

11

Forcing her eyes open, Bexley squeezed them shut again as light flooded her room. Trying to roll over to her nightstand pushed all the air from her lungs, and she let out an airy groan. Why was her room full of light? She struggled to sit up and lean against the headboard, body aching and her mind in a fog.

Finally gripping her phone, she saw it was almost eleven in the morning.

"I never sleep in," she muttered as her stomach growled.

After Evan left last night, she got up, bolted the door, took a shower, and collapsed in bed without eating. Now, she was starved.

Standing on wobbly legs, her whole body ached from being thrown around, kicked, pistol-whipped, and lashed to a chair.

She shuffled to the kitchen for some water then settled into her favorite recliner. Unlocking her phone, Evan's name and number flashed on the screen.

"Huh, I forgot about that."

Her smile grew at the memory of how amazing he had been.

Each time he touched her he had stated his intentions, and

she had great appreciation for that. No money, no phone, and stranded at the hospital, he had come to her rescue.

She scrolled through her contacts and decided on Chinese to be delivered. Grocery shopping had been the next thing to do on her list yesterday. All she had in the fridge was some string cheese, fruit, and juice.

As she decided on what to order, she ignored the calorie content and unhealthy grease and oil as the numbers rolled around in her mind.

Groaning, she punched in the number, eager to order the cream cheese wontons and calorie-laden chicken and lo mein. Tomorrow she would return to a strict health regimen, but today she deserved a treat. On the third ring, her doorbell made her jump as she hung up the phone.

She was never jumpy or scared. Fear wasn't something she allowed to plague her, but right now, she felt herself losing control.

Was it her attacker from yesterday?

Oh, good grief. That man wouldn't ring the doorbell.

Loud knocking continued, and she forced herself from the seat and quietly to the window. Reggie stood on the porch, pounding on the door. Bexley made her way over and unbolted it.

"Hey."

Reggie gasped. "Bexley? What happened?"

Bexley frowned at Reggie's wide eyes. "How did you ... why're you here?"

"It's all over the news."

"*I'm* all over the news?" Bexley clutched her chest. "How ... I mean, my name is all over the news?"

"I saw it this morning and rushed over once I finally got someone to cover for me. Why didn't you call?" Reggie pushed herself into the house.

Bexley sighed as she closed and latched the door. "Honestly, I just got up. Last night I was a little overwhelmed and didn't have my phone ..." she trailed off as Reggie did a visual sweep. "Look, I appreciate you coming over, but I'm fine."

Reggie huffed. "I know fine, and this isn't it." She pointed at Bexley's face. "Tell me everything. Are you in danger? Do you need protection?"

"I'm not sure if I'm supposed to tell you anything, and I doubt I need protection." Bexley let out a grunt as she sat down. "I'm just bruised."

Reggie sat next to her on the couch. "Bex, I can help."

Another ring of her doorbell had her struggling to her feet and Reggie yanking her gun free.

"Now what?' She mumbled as Reggie stood at the window.

"Six-two white guy that looks like he can bench 250 without breaking a sweat is on your porch. Aviators, cropped hair, and a five o'clock shadow. Sound familiar?" Reggie turned with a smile. "Is that why you didn't need my help last night? You had help?"

Bexley eased back to the couch with a grunt. "Just a friend, and yes, he was there to help me last night."

"Hello. And who are you?" Reggie's smooth voice rang out.

Bex looked up to see Evan making his way inside.

"Bexley? You okay?"

She nodded.

Evan turned to Reggie. "And you are?"

"Reggie White." She holstered her weapon. "I don't believe I got your name."

"Evan Mitchell."

"And you know Bexley how?"

"He's part of the TRT. His team helped out last night."

Reggie's eyes cut to her for only a moment. "It's nice of you to come check on her."

Evan nodded. "*You're* Reggie?"

"Yes, friend and former co-worker." Reggie crossed her arms, glaring at Bexley. "I was surprised to find out what happened on the news when I never received a phone call last night."

Bexley grimaced. "I was at the hospital and I—"

"You were at the hospital?" Reggie dropped her arms.

"Doc said she's fine. Nothing's broken."

"Good to know," Reggie mumbled.

Evan turned with a steely glare. "My boss is on his way."

"Why?"

"We need to talk about getting some protection. Your name is out there."

"About that, who leaked my name? How does anyone know about me being involved?"

"I don't know." Evan's jaw clenched. "But seeing how you escaped twice now, I think you might need to consider protective custody."

"Twice? What does that mean?"

Bexley sighed as Reggie stepped between them. "It means the guy that did all this had other plans, and I apparently messed them up."

"What? Then I'm staying."

Evan huffed. "She's got to go somewhere, not be here where anyone can find her."

"Then she's coming with me." Reggie squared off with Evan. "She's my friend."

"Reggie, you know you can't take off right now." Bexley stood once more, attempting to divert the tone of the conversation. "I'm surprised you're even in town."

"My team has a secure office downtown."

Reggie crossed her arms and glared at Evan. "Then why is she here instead of there?"

"There was no reason to think her name had been released or that she was in any danger."

Bexley huffed. "Okay, look, I'm not going anywhere."

"What?" Evan and Reggie spoke in unison.

Her gaze cut to Evan. "After everything that happened, I don't think that guy wants anything to do with me. Really."

Evan stood silent, obviously not as convinced.

"I can stay."

"You have a job." Bexley focused on Reggie. "I appreciate everyone's concern, but this isn't some personal vendetta. There's no reason for him to want anything to do with me. He's probably left the country by now."

"You don't know that." Evan's stern voice sounded. "In fact, no one knows where he is. It would be smart to take precautions."

"That's it. I'm staying. I've got vacation time—"

"Regg, you know you can't take it during this time of year. Besides, if anyone found out it's because of me, you'd be ousted as well. I think you're all blowing this out of proportion. I'm obviously not the reason he was at the mall the other day."

Reggie started pacing.

"We need to talk." Evan pushed into her space. "Now."

Bexley pulled Reggie's arm toward the door. "If something comes up, I'll give you a call. But I think I'm good. Why don't you go back to work? I know this isn't your day off."

"It's not, but after I saw the report, I convinced Marcos to cover me." Reggie pulled to a stop in the doorway. Her eyes cut to Evan for a moment, then back to Bexley. "Call me if you need some help. I'm serious. I can take time if I need to."

She smiled at her friend. "I appreciate it. Thanks."

Reggie nodded. "You better call, Bex. I mean it." Her eyes cut over Bexley's shoulder. "I'll be seeing you around, Evan." Then she turned and headed out the door.

EVAN'S SMILE vanished as the woman left. Reggie White, he'd have Danica run that name and get some background. She sure was pushy and seemed to be protective of Bexley.

"So, what is it you need to talk about?" Bexley collapsed in the chair with a grimace.

"I think you should consider taking a vacation or something." She rolled her eyes. "He was there for the bank, not me."

"Is that what he said?"

"Basically." She shrugged. "Something about the bank, needing—something …" She trailed off, her focus on her hands.

He studied the bandages still wrapped around one wrist and the brace on the other. The sound of a car door diverted his attention, and he went to the window. Buck headed up the sidewalk and he opened the door.

"She okay?"

He shrugged at Buck's question. Honestly, she didn't look okay. The bruising had worsened, and that black-and-blue cut on her head was spidery with stitches.

Stepping back, he let Buck through.

"I take it you're Evan's boss." Bexley stood gingerly to shake Buck's hand.

"I am. Buck Thompson. Have a seat, Ms. Bowers."

Bexley's eyes cut to Evan a moment before going back to Buck. She winced as she sat, gripping her hands in front. He took the couch, and Buck sat on the loveseat.

"Ms. Bowers, I have a few questions."

"I told the agent everything—"

"The police?"

She nodded. "Well, two men. One was a detective, and the other was an FBI agent. I can't remember his name."

Buck nodded. "Okay, but I'd like to hear it from your point of view."

She sighed. "Once we got to the building, he was on the phone, yelling about how he couldn't get it right now. I asked if I could help him get whatever it was, but he said I was the reason for his downfall?"

Evan fisted his hands.

"Think it through. Close your eyes and tell me what happened from the moment you got into that SUV." Buck pulled out his phone.

Closing her eyes, she took a few breaths. "He talked a lot. On the phone maybe … no, an earpiece. He couldn't have a phone."

"Why not?" Evan leaned in as she opened her bright green eyes.

"Between driving and the gun, he wouldn't have been able to hold a phone."

"What?"

She groaned. "Look, he was driving, shouting, and shoving a gun in my side. I made a comment, and he hit my head with the butt of the gun. I must've blacked out. I woke as he was pulling my hair to get me out of the SUV."

Evan's face heated at the thought.

"Bexley, do you remember anything he said before you passed out?"

"No, I know he was talking, but I don't really remember words." She frowned as she rubbed her temple.

"Okay, then when you woke up?" Buck's gray eyes narrowed.

"He shoved me into a chair. Mentally, I knew several ways to get away from him, but physically ... I couldn't." She paused. "He strapped me in, then I lost visual. I remember seeing a lot of machine parts, figured I was at a scrap yard or machine shop. I could hear him yelling about his plan and the fact he needed what was there. . . "

"There? You mean the bank?"

She nodded at Buck.

"What did it smell like?"

Her eyes cut to Evan. "What?"

"Bombers often have a certain chemical they use as their signature. We retrieved a lot of C-4. I wonder if there was another chemical he wanted to use elsewhere, and he took it with him."

"It just smelled like diesel and oil. I don't remember anything else."

"You said he got his revenge?" Buck frowned.

She winced. "Yeah, I was asking him why he was doing all this, and he said he was paying me back for the loss of his team. He said I was his downfall."

"His downfall?"

"Yeah." Her gaze dropped to her hands.

Evan gripped his fingers together to keep from reaching out.

"I think it would be wise to take precautions." Buck's gaze narrowed as Bexley shook her head.

"You really think he cares about coming after me?"

"We don't know. That's why you need to be in protective custody." Evan barely controlled the tone in his voice.

Her eyebrows furrowed, her jaw set.

"Well, if you do change your mind, we'd be glad to offer some help, just until he's caught." Buck stood to leave.

Wait, what? Evan glared at Buck. What was he doing? Bexley needed protection. Her name was everywhere.

"Like I said, I appreciate your concern, but I know how protection details work. I don't plan on putting myself in that situation." Her gaze cut to him. "I would, however, like my gun back."

Evan shrugged. "I'll see what I can do. Surely you have a backup."

"Of course." Pushing herself to stand, she motioned to them. "I think we're good."

Buck offered a card. "Here's my number if you need anything."

"I have Evan's number, but thanks." She took it as Buck gave him a knowing glance.

"Be safe. Call if you need anything." Buck headed to the door and, after taking a quick look outside, marched to his car.

"Bexley, you sure?"

Every alarm was going off in Evan's head about leaving her alone. She could easily be the target of this terrorist. He and Buck would be discussing this later.

She turned with a sigh. "I'm fine. I know I don't look it, but I'm good." She motioned to the door. "Thanks for stopping by."

Not able to come up with a reason to stay, he filed out the

Fighter

door and to the road. Buck's truck was still parked next to his SUV and he slid into the passenger seat.

"You want to tell me why we're not taking her into protective custody?"

Buck shrugged. "She doesn't want to go. Besides, she's right. We don't have any proof she's a target." He rubbed the scruff on his chin. "I am going to look into the bank angle. We need to get that sorted out."

"I thought Homeland was doing the sorting?" He chuckled at Buck's frown.

"It happened to one of our own. Arlo Androssier is a dangerous and wanted man. I want to know why he's here and what he's after."

Evan let out a breath. "I'll meet you back at the office."

"Sure."

He slid from the truck and back to his vehicle. Sitting behind the wheel, he tapped his fingers several times on the gear shift. Glancing back to the house, he saw the curtains move and chuckled. She was watching.

Maybe he should stay. Just for a little while.

His phone beeped.

You can go. I don't need a babysitter.

He smirked.

Just taking my time.

Well, don't. BTW, I've got my backup ready.

Good. Call if you need anything.

Pushing the SUV in gear, he paused as a silver Range Rover pulled into her driveway. A man in a suit and tie rushed to the door, and Evan shoved the gearshift in park.

12

Bexley stood slack-jawed at Tennison standing in front of her, his cheeks bright red.

"Bexley? What happened? Are you okay? You don't look okay."

"I ..." Too shocked to answer, she stepped back as he reached out, his brows furrowed.

"Do you need help? I can move some protection to your house."

"That won't be necessary."

Her eyes cut behind Tennison at the sound of Evan's voice. Arms crossed, Evan's jaw tightened as he glared from under the bill of his hat.

"And you are?" Tennison turned with a growl.

She stepped onto the porch. "This is Evan. He and his team—"

"Evan Mitchell. And you are?"

"Tennison Andrews."

Evan stood waiting as Tennison took a step forward. "Bexley and I are former ... co-workers."

This can't be happening.

"Bexley has chosen to stay here. If she needs help, my team—"

"I have a twenty-man team at my disposal. I can help with protection." Tennison turned to her with a smile. "Let's go inside, and we can discuss a team for you. I'm assuming you'll want Reggie to lead."

"I don't need a team. Thanks." Her face on fire, she finally locked eyes with Evan. "I appreciate your concern, but he's okay. You can go."

"I can wait," he murmured.

"If she said to go, I'd listen." Tennison once more turned to Evan.

"Okay, look." She stepped between them, facing Evan. "I'm good here, and I appreciate your help. I told you, I'm not going anywhere, and no one will be coming here for protection." She turned to Tennison. "I appreciate your concern, but I'm okay."

"I can see that you're okay. Let's go inside and discuss this." Tennison's smile gone, he took hold of Bexley's elbow.

She yanked back, her hand fisting. "Don't do that again," she muttered.

"I think it's time you leave."

She could feel Evan behind her. "I ... I think you should go."

Tennison's hazel eyes darkened as his hands clenched at his sides. "Bexley, we need to talk."

"Call her," Evan gritted.

Tennison's eyes never left hers. "I'll call you tonight. We need to discuss some things."

Unable to come up with a response, she only nodded and stepped to the side, away from both men.

Evan didn't budge as Tennison passed him on the porch steps.

Hands shaking, she held her sides as Tennison's Range Rover backed out from her driveway and sped away.

Evan turned, silent as he watched her.

"You—you can go too," she murmured before retreating to

her door.

"Bexley."

Stepping inside, she held the door's edge.

"If he comes back, call me."

"I don't need your help with him. I can handle it myself."

He frowned. "You shouldn't have to." Stepping to the door, he shoved his hands in his pockets and looked like he was about to speak, then exhaled instead. "Call any time."

"Thanks."

She watched him descend the steps and slide into the large pickup truck across the street.

"Did you find the leak?"

After his earlier interaction with a supposed co-worker of Bexley's, Evan's irritation rang through as Buck frowned up at him.

"Problem?" Buck asked.

"Besides the fact that everyone knows Bexley Bowers was involved in what happened yesterday?"

Jeff took a spot next to Evan at the kitchen island. The team waited there, file folders and paperwork covering the top.

"Easy. Is there a problem at Bexley's?"

Evan cut his eyes to Jeff. "Let's just discuss the situation," he mumbled.

"Well, from what I've gathered, it was the hostage."

Evan's jaw dropped as Buck stared right through him. "What?"

"The woman she exchanged herself for. She went on the news to ask Bex to come forward and that she wants to thank her for saving her life."

"She heard me call her name," Evan muttered, clenching his jaw as he fisted his hand and slammed it on the island.

"I've talked to her. She's agreed to keep quiet, but she does want to see Bexley," Buck grumbled.

Evan shook his head. Bexley was in danger. That sixth sense from his Navy days was coming back like a drop in his stomach. He was never wrong. Well, usually.

And now with that Tennison guy hanging around ...

"Where's Danica?" Buck looked around the island.

"She told me she won't be here till tomorrow morning," Jeff answered.

"Oh." Buck narrowed his eyes at no one.

Evan surveyed the group, Danica indeed missing. That was odd. Since he started, she was always present and involved.

"Let's start with the warehouse." Sergio laid out several stacks of pictures. "It had everything you could want to build a bomb. We found more C-4 packed into the barrels, which makes me think they had something more than the mall planned."

"And Arlo?" Evan grunted as he sifted through the pictures.

"Right, Arlo Androssier. Master explosives expert and arms dealer. Tops the food chain, or so he thinks."

Evan smirked at Sergio's commentary. Sergio was the only married man in the group and had been with the team a few months longer than him. As the resident computer wizard, he could dig up information on anyone, anywhere, not to mention his skills as a former SWAT team member.

Sergio continued. "According to Homeland and the FBI, Arlo has dozens of aliases; that's how he got into the States. He's on several watch lists, and the scary part is, no one can find him."

"You thinking the port?" Haiden chimed in.

"Yeah, that's the most logical place for him to have entered. Maybe if we can find his way in, we can find his way out too." Evan nodded at Haiden.

"But why the mall? He had a crew of mercenaries with him. They go after high-end targets that pay their bankroll." Sergio looked around the table.

"Did you ever consider it's simply about money?"

They all looked to Jeff.

"No, not really." Buck leaned into the island.

Jeff shrugged. "Well, considering there were no such targets at the mall in the middle of the day, it seems more than likely they were going after money in the bank. Maybe they need the money for something."

"But what?" Sergio looked around the island. "It's a small branch, there can't be that much cash there."

"Were they expecting any large deposits or transfers?" Evan asked.

"Not that we know about."

"That's something we can check into. As far as federal help, Homeland has nothing to give us. Right now, it's being labeled as a terrorist attack. Arlo has ties to Syria as well as other terrorist-sympathetic nations. My buddy at Homeland says he'll try and keep us updated about where the investigation is going. If this was a planned soft-target attack, then there'll be more, and we'll need to be on high alert."

Evan nodded. His mind wandered to Bexley. Having a wanted man like Arlo around who already blamed her for what happened at the mall ... He sighed. Yeah, she needed protection.

"Let's start with the port. Call the Coast Guard and see if they know of any ships arriving from Arlo's last known location. He could've come in and hopped a transport to Dallas with little trouble. Also, how does he get out? Any foreign ships headed out soon that would be friendly with him?" Buck ordered.

"I'll do it." Sergio grabbed his laptop and rushed upstairs to the computers they had set up in the loft.

"I want someone on the fingerprints from the warehouse. I want to know without a doubt that everyone is accounted for. Prints to bodies, I want it all tied up."

"I'm on it." Jeff grabbed the file folder that had the prints in it.

"That leaves me with what?" Haiden leaned into the island, looking to Buck.

"Homeland is busy with the money trail. So why don't you

investigate known associates? Why is he here? We need to know where he's been and who he's been talking to. Hopefully, that will give us an idea if more attacks are imminent."

Haiden nodded and headed upstairs with Sergio to the computers.

"Something on your mind?"

Evan's gaze went to Buck. "I just have a feeling she's in over her head."

Buck narrowed his eyes as he leaned into the island. "Well, usually we go with gut instincts. But right now, we've got nothing to lead us to Bexley as a specific target. Besides, she's not a normal citizen. She's trained. She can protect herself. If it weren't for her quick thinking at the mall, Arlo would've blown it all up with all those civilians inside."

"You really think that's what this is? A soft target assassination?"

"Not really." Buck huffed. "But this isn't our case to begin with. We do the groundwork, and the police and feds do the rest."

Evan chuckled. "Then why are we looking into Arlo?"

Buck's eyes darkened. "I don't want him in our city. The more people looking for him, the better. We've got time in our schedule to do some studying on this. Unless you just feel the need for another training venture."

"Not at the moment, no." Evan crossed his arms. "What do you want me to do?"

"I want you to dig deeper into Bexley's background."

"You're joking. Why? We've already done a search."

"I want to know what you think of her, her character, her strength."

Evan shrugged. "I think we've all seen both from yesterday."

Buck nodded, his gaze narrowing. "Danica wants her on the team."

"What?" Evan's jaw clenched as he straightened. "She told me she wasn't going to mention that."

"Why does it bother you?"

"She's too green. I mean, yeah, there's training in protective services, but nothing like what we do. She's never seen the kind of action we deal with every day."

"She did yesterday."

Evan sighed and leaned back against the counter. Why would Buck even consider hiring someone with so little experience?

"I'm not saying it'll happen, but I am interested. Do some digging on her previous job. I'll speak to her former employer, find out more about her skills. Danica's right—we're short, and another woman would help her out."

"Danica is different. She's tough and trained."

"You don't think Bexley is tough enough?"

Evan shook his head. "She is, but she's not trained."

"Training comes easier than strength and character. Don't discount her yet—she stood next to you in a firefight and gave herself up in exchange for a hostage."

With a huff, Evan headed toward the stairwell. "I'm going to call the bank and find out about the deposit or possible transfer situation."

The conversation was ridiculous. Even if Bexley was healthy and uninjured, the idea of her joining their group was ludicrous. Her skill set was protection, not action. Everything she knew was reactionary training. She probably knew how to handle a weapon, but other than that—

"Good grief," he muttered as he sat down in front of a computer.

His focus was in the wrong place again, and he had to find a way to shift it. Finding Arlo would cinch everything up and give Buck time to reconsider hiring someone with little field experience.

And Bexley—well, Buck was right. She had handled herself well yesterday. She showed courage and strength by standing up to Arlo and trading herself for that hostage.

He sighed. So much for focus.

13

Searching through the copied database from the bank branch, he hunted for a specific alias, the name he'd been waiting to find. As he highlighted the name and box number, an unexpected name popped up.

"Bexley Bowers."

His mind shifted as he paced. The reason behind the attack, the reason he was de-railed. Bowers was key. His mission failed. The men scattered. All of it, her fault.

According to the news, she was released from the hospital, so she escaped his bomb.

"You are intriguing, Bexley Bowers," he murmured to no one.

Maybe she was the way to get what he came for. After all, it wasn't coincidence that put them together in that bookstore.

All the bank information and safety deposit boxes were going to be sent to another location in two days. Location change would mean more security, a new plan in a new location. That was time he didn't have. He must act now.

The next team was set to arrive in the morning. As he paced the room, another option floated through his mind. Yes, she could do it. First, he needed more information.

"Let's see who you really are, Bexley. I have a feeling you'll be the answer to all this."

SITTING in the back office with Jeff, Evan frowned at the pages in front of him.

"What now?"

He shrugged at Jeff. "I've not been on this side of things. I'm used to following orders, doing the job." He sat down the pages on the couch. "Why is Buck so intent on this anyway? I get there could be more attacks, but the cops have this covered."

Jeff leaned back, crossing an ankle over his knee. "Buck sees this as a teaching opportunity."

Staring at the opposite wall, Evan couldn't shake the vision of Tennison holding on to Bexley's elbow and her jumping back.

"Ev?"

Focusing his eyes on Jeff, Evan then rolled his shoulders to ease tension.

"What happened?"

Evan shrugged. "When?"

"After Buck left. He called as he was leaving and said she was good. But the way you're acting, something else is going on."

"Just drop it. It's nothing."

"From the look on your face, it's not nothing. Is there something else we need to look into?"

Evan shook his head. "No, probably nothing," he mumbled.

He hoped it was nothing.

Danica made her way inside the office, blowing out a heavy breath.

Jeff stared at him for a second longer before putting his gaze on Danica. "You're early. I didn't think you were coming back till tomorrow."

"Yeah, well, plans change." She tossed her bag inside the door.

Fighter

Snagging the file folder from Jeff, she dropped down on the couch next to Evan. "So, do we know why he's here? Do we think Bexley is now a target?"

Haiden appeared, making his way into the room, taking a seat beside her.

Jeff shrugged. "As far as a target, I mean, it doesn't sit right with me. There's no reason for him to be interested in her just because she got in a lucky punch and got away."

"Wait, she punched this Arlo guy?" Her mouth dropped.

"Yeah, hard," Evan muttered.

Jeff cleared his throat. "She's refusing to be in protective custody, but Buck and Evan are concerned."

Danica's eyes met Evan's for a split second before studying the papers she took from Jeff. "Well, did you guys figure out what the main target is? And what it has to do with the bank? Were they expecting a deposit or something?"

"No, they weren't expecting anything, and it wasn't a normal pickup day." Evan stood to pace.

Pushing the need to call and check on Bexley to the back of his mind, Evan wondered just who Tennison was in her life. Although based on her reaction to Tennison pulling her elbow, Evan had a pretty good idea.

"Buck's been on the phone trying to get some info together about Arlo. He's a ghost. Although he's on a few no-fly lists and a terrorist watch, he's been silent for years."

"Okay, let's think this out." She leaned forward on her knees. "He takes his crew and kidnaps a bunch of people in the most high-end part of the mall. Why?"

"The bank. He needs the money," Jeff answered.

"Okay, I get that. So, Bexley and Evan thwart his plans and escape, taking out a few of his men. Then, once we go in with SWAT, we take out even more men, leaving him alone?"

Jeff shook his head. "I went through the fingerprints and bodies. We're missing three."

"Maybe that's who he was talking to in the SUV." Haiden had his focus on Danica.

Danica looked to Haiden. "What?"

"Yeah, when we visited earlier, Bexley mentioned Arlo speaking to someone. It had to be an earpiece. He had the gun on her and driving," Evan explained.

She nodded. "So, one of the men got in touch with him, that's one piece. Did she see him at the warehouse?"

Evan shook his head. "Not according to Bexley."

"Okay, she gets away from the explosion and lives. But you're right. That's a thin piece of ice to stand on if it's revenge. He's got to have another agenda. Guys like him are looking for money, guns, or something like that."

Buck stepped into the office, his focus on Danica. "Everything good?"

"Yes, sir."

"Good. Did Jeff read you in?"

"Yeah, but we're missing a lot. What's the target? Why's he here?" She tapped her lip a moment. "We need more information to determine what his focus is. Unless you actually think it's Bexley."

Buck shrugged. "I've not ruled that out. But she's certainly not his reason for being in the country."

"Money?"

Buck shrugged. "Maybe this will help." He handed a file to Danica. "Here's the profile the CIA made on Arlo five years ago when a CIA mole made its way into his organization."

"Wait." Jeff stood. "You mean we already had him in our sights, and someone failed?"

"Nope, the CIA was there simply for recon purposes. The entire group was set to be dismantled and arrested, but he beat them to it."

Evan shook his head. "He, as in Arlo, destroyed his own group?"

"Yep." Buck leaned a shoulder against the wall. "He's

paranoid, with a lot of brainpower. He figured someone was spying on him, which they were, so he took them all out. Suspicious doesn't even begin to describe him."

"Great. Guy's paranoid and willing to dismantle his entire group," Evan mumbled.

More bad news for Bexley and her safety. Leaving the room, he headed to his truck. If she wasn't going to accept protection, then he'd have to be ready for the next attack.

His gut churned as he slid into the seat. Chest tight, he started the truck with a grunt.

Years of training and operations overseas had given him more than a sixth sense. Facts were facts. Arlo was a dangerous man, and Bexley had put herself in the middle of what he wanted. Evan wasn't going to let her be a target.

"God, give her some protection if I can't get there in time," he mumbled.

14

Bexley sighed as she stared at the movie playing on TV. Five o'clock and she was already beat, exhausted from a long day of ignoring phone calls and news reporters at her door.

Who had released her name to the public?

Mindlessly staring at the screen, she was startled by the phone ringing.

"What now?" she murmured.

The screen displayed a blocked caller, and she hit *end*.

"Probably another reporter wanting a statement."

With all this attention, she needed a PR person if she were going to get any rest.

The phone buzzed again, the same blocked caller on the screen. Annoyed, she answered.

"Look, I'm not interested in an interview—"

"Bexley Bowers."

Her name hissed through the phone with a familiar tone. She jumped up, her stomach swirling and her heart pounding.

"I ... I would say your name, but I have no idea what it is."

"Oh, I'm sure your friends know who I am."

"What friends?" She was breathless as she gripped her side, working to control the pain radiating through her body.

"I'm sure you have friends listening in. I just wanted to have a chat, learn more about you, Bexley."

A shudder rocked her body. "Why ... why are you calling? Why did you blow up the mall?"

"You know, I've been reading a lot about you. You have a devastating past, one that connects us."

She huffed. "There's nothing that connects us."

"Oh, but you see, I lost my parents as a teenager as well. I know the pain you've struggled with. I've struggled too."

Stifling her groan, she shoved on her tennis shoes and pulled her sidearm to her chest, awkwardly holding it with her left hand. "Oh really? How did your parents die?"

"War, but that's not why I called." His clipped answer hung in the air. "I want to know who you run to when there's no one else."

The lights went out and she sprinted down the hallway, locking her bedroom door.

"Bexley? Do you have an answer for me?"

"No one. I can protect myself."

After slamming and locking the bathroom door, she angled herself at the corner, aimed and ready for someone to come through. Adrenaline surging, her hands shook as the reminder of the injury to her side flared.

"I'm sure you think you can."

The echo of a door sounded.

"But the thing is, that help you offered, I'm more than willing to accept it now."

"Sorry, too late. You should've taken me up on the offer yesterday." With that, she hung up and dialed Evan's number.

"Hey—"

"He's here."

"On our way. Are you okay?"

"I'm in the back bathroom. He called, then the lights cut out and—"

"Bex? Breathe, we'll be there in five minutes."

Fighter

She huffed. "You can't get anywhere in Dallas in five minutes."

He chuckled, the sound easing the pounding of her heart. "I was out driving around."

"You were checking on me? I told you—"

"It sounds like I was right."

A loud crash and she almost dropped the phone as a scream slipped out.

"Bex?"

"Just get here!" She threw the phone down, using both hands to hold the weapon ready. Dizziness rippled her vision. "Not now, just focus."

Easing herself to the ground, she leaned against the wall as the noises ceased. Silence filled the room. No more sound came through the phone.

Swallowing hard, she did her best to stay alert as fear and pain surged through her body.

EVAN PARKED OUTSIDE and rushed to the house, surveying the area and lack of movement. Gun drawn, he turned on the flashlight and shone through the early evening shadows inside the living room. Entering, he cleared the rooms one by one, noting overturned furniture and destruction throughout the house.

Making his way to the back, he found her bedroom door barely hanging on the hinges, the window wide open. Clearing the closet and under the bed, he knocked on the bathroom door.

"Bexley? Bex, it's me."

A shuffling sounded through the door, and then the snap of the lock disengaging. The door cracked open, and Bexley stood there holding a gun to her chest.

"Did you ... was he here?"

He nodded. "I've seen no one. The door was open, and that window." His phone buzzed. "Yeah?"

"You clear?"

"Clear." He hung up on Buck and pushed at the door.

Her eyes darted to his. "I'm fine," she whispered.

He only nodded.

Jeff appeared in the hallway, breathing heavy. "Buck has the outside. Let me know when you're ready to go, I'll cover you."

"Thanks." He looked back to Bexley. "Get a bag together. You're staying at our office until this thing clears up."

Her jaw tightened as she lowered her gun, shoving it into the waistband of her pants.

"You sure you want to do that? I thought you were a response team, not protection." Her wide eyes flashed at him for only a second before landing on the remnants of her bedroom door with a sigh.

"I think we can handle it. If not, I'm sure you can correct us."

"Not funny, Evan," she whispered.

"Wasn't trying to be funny, Bex," he whispered back.

She nodded slightly, her shoulders slumping as she stared at her torn-apart room.

"I'll be back in a sec." He checked the room one last time before stepping into the hall to give her some space.

"She okay?" Jeff frowned as he stared at the remnants of the living room.

"Yeah, I guess. I'm not sure she would admit otherwise," Evan muttered. "Find anything?"

"Buck said the breaker box was cut. Professionally enough that there probably won't be any prints or leads. This is interesting, though."

Evan followed Jeff to the kitchen. Jeff shone his flashlight on the wall next to the dining room table. Jagged letters scrawled "Until Next Time" in the sheetrock.

"This is ... odd. From the information Buck had, Arlo's a man with a plan. So why go after Bexley?" Jeff turned to him.

Evan shrugged. "Revenge?"

Jeff frowned. "I spoke with Homeland, and they mentioned Arlo's men accessed the bank computers and got the teller drawers. But other than that, it was a complete bust. He didn't get enough money or information to be worth a mercenary's time."

"What did he get off the computers?" Evan clenched his jaw, doing his best to focus on Jeff and not rush back to the bedroom to help Bexley.

"The info they received wasn't personal, like socials and stuff. At least, that's what Homeland is telling me. That was the first thing they checked. They're supposed to let me know exactly what was accessed." Jeff swung his flashlight around the room with a huff. "We need to get his plan down. He's got us running in circles so far."

The red and blue lights flashing outside the living room window caught Evan's eye. "Police?"

"Yeah. Buck says he can smooth it out if Bexley comes willingly."

"That's good." Evan wanted her protected and not in police custody.

Swallowing hard, he paced the room, angry at himself for not making her come with him.

"You can't make her do something she doesn't want to do."

He spun. "What?"

Jeff chuckled. "Look, it's clear you think this is your fault. But if she didn't want to leave, you couldn't make her."

"She should've realized how bad this could become. We all saw this coming."

"Maybe you and Buck." Jeff shrugged. "I didn't think anything of it. She has a point. Arlo is guided by money, guns, information, even revenge on someone that stabbed him in the back. But just because she got away from him doesn't mean he'd drop everything, his original plan, just to come scare her. That's pushing the bounds of sanity."

"Yeah, well, I don't think he's all that sane."

"You could be right," Jeff mumbled as he studied the wall once again, snapping a picture on his phone.

Peering down the hallway, Evan sighed.

God, give me the strength to protect her. Please let her see how dangerous this is and trust us.

15

Bexley stared at the hanging door, the cool fall breeze from the broken window pushing at her clammy skin. He had come for her, just as Evan predicted.

She opened drawers, grabbing handfuls of clothes to throw inside her duffle. She paused at the unfolded mess. Part of her wanted to dump it out and start over. But now, after her world crashing and her life anew, she felt almost weightless, as if none of this really mattered. And in all actuality, it didn't.

Finding some jeans and a long-sleeved shirt, she stepped back into the bathroom to change.

Leaning against the sink, she closed her eyes. Pain and anger washed through her body.

Why would he come after her? He said he wanted her help. What kind of help? What was happening here?

Blowing out a deep breath, she finished packing her toiletries and took them back to the bedroom, shoving them into her duffle bag. Her energy was bottoming out as the adrenaline pulsed from her system. If she didn't sit down soon, she'd collapse.

"You ready?"

Hiding her surprise at Evan's sudden appearance, she

clenched her jaw. "Yeah, I'm done."

"You need to make a call?"

Her eyes narrowed as Evan stood there watching, completely unreadable.

Did he mean Tennison?

"No, no calls."

Evan reached around and took the duffle from the bed. "Then let's go."

Instinctively yanking her arm back as he grazed it with his hand, she ignored his heavy sigh.

"Buck's cleared it with the police. You just have to let them know what happened and that you're agreeing to stay with us for now."

"Yeah, I know how it works."

Great. Being protected instead of being the one doing the protecting. What could go wrong?

God, give me some grace and forethought tonight. Thank You for Your protection, and please remind me that You're here with me.

BEXLEY LEANED HER HEAD BACK, her body drained. Evan had taken an extended route with a lot of turns and back alleys, probably making sure they weren't followed. During the quiet time, she debated if staying with the TRT was the right thing to do. They weren't a protection agency, rather a team similar to SWAT.

They pulled up to a building with a small storefront. Sitting in the SUV, she noticed the car that had followed them from her home take a right turn into the alleyway next to the building. Moments later, Evan got a text. A two-man team, huh? It seemed the TRT knew a little something about protection after all.

Evan opened her door, the crisp air whipping at her hair as she slid to the ground with a huff.

"You okay?"

"Great," she mumbled.

He guided her to the large door. The mirrored glass reflected enough of her image that she combed back the messy tendrils with her fingers. A beep sounded, and they stepped inside.

At first glance, the office appeared ordinary and small. The foyer was a subdued gray color with yellow and green highlights on the wall and on the couch pillows.

After passing a tall, oak-stained desk in the corner, she followed him down a small hallway that held a few offices, then they came to a door. Evan put in a code and then swiped a card before the door opened.

"Come on in."

The room opened to a large living and kitchen area. A red sectional took up most of the living room, along with the large ottoman and big screen TV.

"What's this? I thought I was staying at your office?"

"Well, this is the back of the office. Three of us are here at all times. We switch off weeks." He led her inside and she stood at a large, stained, concrete island. "You'll be staying with Danica in the upstairs loft. The rest of us stay on the lower level."

"How many of you are there?"

"Right now, six, counting Buck."

She simply nodded, enjoying the happiness that seemed to light his face from just being here. He must love his job. A twinge of jealousy hit her heart.

He motioned to the dimly lit hallway running underneath the stairwell. "That hallway leads to the men's rooms, and upstairs is where you and Danica will be."

"Danica is the only woman?"

He nodded. "Hey, Jeff?"

A man came in from the downstairs hallway, below the staircase. He was busy removing the tactical vest as he headed for the kitchen. He had bleach-blonde hair swept back and bright blue eyes. His pointed features matched his long limbs and lean physique.

"Jeff, this is Bexley Bowers. If you can stay here, I'll go get her stuff from the car."

"Sure." Jeff offered his hand as well as a huge smile. "Nice to officially meet you."

"You too." She slid onto the barstool and leaned into the island, noticing Evan had already disappeared.

"Water?"

She took the offered bottle and cracked the seal to take a drink.

"How're ya holding up? Between yesterday and today, I imagine you're about to collapse."

"It's just part of life," she shrugged.

"I'm not sure that's an accurate description." He leaned against the counter, arms crossed. "In your previous line of work, I imagine you've had some close calls. But this is a different kind of action."

She huffed. "Yesterday wasn't exactly a close call."

Three minutes. That's all she had left when Evan arrived.

A shudder pierced her skin. In their line of work, being in danger was just part of the job. However, being kidnapped and strapped to a bomb, well, that wasn't something she had prepared for.

Jeff's voice broke into her thoughts. "You might consider seeing a therapist. What you went through, it's not something you can just shake off."

"I'll be fine," she muttered.

Therapy wasn't a new concept. When she lost her family, she'd gone for years. But it didn't help her find a healthy way to deal with the pain and emptiness.

"You're a lot quieter than I thought you would be."

She raised her eyebrow. "What does that mean?"

Jeff shrugged. "I just expected more of an argument or discussion, I guess."

"Sorry to disappoint."

He let out a chuckle. "That's more like it."

"Like what?"

"Evan just mentioned you could be difficult to communicate with."

"Interesting. So you guys have all talked about me, huh?" She leaned forward on her left arm, hoping to ease the pressure on her side. "So, tell me about Evan and the rest of the team."

"Oh no." He chuckled. "Not my job."

She shrugged. "You've all talked about me. Isn't it fair I learn about each of you?"

"This has nothing to do with fairness. This is about self-preservation. Most of us enjoy our privacy, me included." He grinned, showing perfect white teeth.

"I just don't get any, huh?"

"We had to do our homework on you. I'm sorry if that bothers you, but it's part of the job. You should know that."

"I know, it just doesn't make it easier. " She turned at the sound of Evan coming back inside with her duffle over his shoulder. "I was just hoping for at least a little courtesy."

Jeff grinned as her gaze left Evan and fell back on him. Once Evan disappeared up the stairs, Jeff leaned in.

"Well, if it's stuff on him you want, good luck. I can tell you he's usually a grumpy person from sunup to sundown with little in between that resembles a good mood."

She frowned. "Why?"

Jeff shrugged his shoulders and straightened. "Guess you'll have to ask him."

"Not sure I want to get into that situation."

"I don't know, from what I've been told, you seem to have held your own with him pretty well." Jeff flashed another smile.

"Yeah, well, I don't like to be told what to do."

"I can see that."

He stepped away, pulling out his phone as he sat down in a recliner in the living area. Her gaze bounced around the large open room. The stairwell rested next to the kitchen and led to a hallway and an open loft.

"You good?" Evan's voice echoed in the large room as he walked from under the stairwell to the kitchen.

"Yes, fine," she muttered as she paused to take a drink.

She closed her eyes for a moment as pain surged through her lower back.

"Bexley?"

She waved him off, but felt him next to her, pushing in close.

"What's wrong?"

"I ... I just have a sharp pain moving up my back." She tried to straighten, but the pull made things worse.

"Your muscles are probably knotting up from the hits you took yesterday and the stress of tonight. Go lie down on the couch."

Pain burned through her as she tried to stand, and she crumpled over with a groan.

"I'm going to help you," Evan murmured as he gripped both elbows and led her to the couch. "Now, lay down and stretch out your legs and relax your back into the cushions. Did you fill that prescription from the hospital?"

"No, I ... I don't like to take pills."

"Yeah, well, I think that's about to get tested." His intense blue eyes looked her over as he knelt next to her on the couch.

She ignored his tone and closed her eyes as she tried to relax, stretching her legs out. Raising her right arm, she let out a breath as pain radiated down her back.

"Easy, don't push it. Let me get some ice."

Evan's footsteps echoed as she let her arm down.

"Easy, Bexley."

A force took hold of her wrist and she shot up, wrenching her arm away. Her eyes focused on Jeff, his hands up and confusion on his face.

"What's wrong?"

Evan's voice sounded from behind her as she tried to ease her breathing.

"I was just trying to help. I ..." Jeff's brows furrowed.

"My eyes were closed and I didn't know you were here. I was startled when you grabbed my wrist. I'm sorry." She held her side, slowly leaning over, nauseous. "I think I'm going to be sick."

"Sit down, I'll get you some water."

She barely made it back to the couch before the tears streamed down her face as she held her head.

"Jeff, can you give us a minute?"

Taking deep breaths, Bexley did what she could to control the sobs.

"Bex, hey." Evan was in front of her, that soft voice he used last night calming her. "You're good."

She finally evened out her breathing, wiping her face and flinching at the pain from her cheek.

"Good grief, I'm a mess," she managed to mutter.

"Nah, just having a bad day." He gently patted her knee.

"Try lifetime," she whispered.

Biting her lip, she shook her head, hoping she said it softly enough he didn't hear. The cool, wet water bottle pushed into her hands.

"You move like that, you're going to make things worse."

She only nodded, taking a few sips of water, and trying to ease the knot in her chest. He poured a few pills into her hand, and she frowned.

"What's this?"

"Over-the-counter anti-inflammatory. You need to take it for your muscles and your side."

She reluctantly swallowed them and capped the bottle, squeezing it in her hand.

"I ... I just didn't know he was there. He caught me by surprise. That doesn't happen very often," she muttered.

"No worries. Just take some breaths and relax."

Letting out a breath, she closed her eyes.

God, give me some grace. Please.

16

Bexley focused on the water bottle, taking easy breaths as she contained the constant ache through her body. "I ... I think I should go to bed. I'm beat."

"Come on, I'll help you up the stairs."

"Yeah, great, stairs." She glared as he stood and chuckled.

"Sorry." He flashed that impressive smile, and she shook her head.

As she stood, a moment of dizziness engulfed her. She gripped his arm.

"You need to be careful. That hit to the head, it's going to keep you from moving around too much."

"I'll be fine."

"You say that an awful lot, but that doesn't make it true."

He pushed some hair away from her face. She flinched, pulling back as his brow furrowed.

"Don't look at me like that." She rolled her eyes, pulling her hand from his arm.

"Like what?"

"Like that. It's involuntary, okay?"

His lips parted a moment before he closed them. "Okay. Let's go."

Standing at the bottom of the stairwell, she sighed.

"Want me to carry you?"

She turned to retort, but his serious expression changed her mind. "It's okay, I can do it."

Probably.

Taking a breath, she made her way up the steps, stiffening her back and gripping the rail with her left hand. She felt his steady presence behind her, guiding her to her bedroom for the next few days.

"Here's your bed, the bathroom is through there. I would suggest keeping away from Danica's stuff. She can be a little protective."

She nodded, then noticed her duffle bag on the floor on the empty side of the room. Two beds lined the walls on opposite sides, desks, dressers, and bookshelves also on either side.

"Protective, huh? That's interesting." She turned, a smirk on her face.

"What does that mean?"

"Just that you seem to have your own protective instincts flying off of you."

He grinned as she worked to get her coat off.

"Here." He stepped in and helped her slide it off as she grimaced, then carefully pulled her brace through the sleeve. "Shoulders still sore?"

"Yeah, I ... I guess I thought my side would be the only thing hurting today, but my whole body aches." She carefully sat on the chair by the empty desk and blew out a deep breath, closing her eyes.

"Bexley, you can't rush this. You need to give yourself time to heal. No exercise or running around, just rest."

"Sure, that sounds great." She huffed as she looked up to see him watching her again. This time, she could tell he had something else on his mind. "What?"

He shrugged as his hands pushed into his pockets, and she rolled her eyes.

Fighter

"I'm too tired. If you have a question, ask. Otherwise, leave. I want to go to sleep."

He pulled the chair from the other desk in front of her and sat. Leaning in, he rested his arms on his knees. "Why did you do it?"

"Do what?" She turned her head, stifling a yawn.

"Why did you take that woman's place?"

She paused for a moment, searching for the right words that wouldn't make her seem crazy or anymore pitiful than she felt.

"I ... I don't know, I just felt like I needed to help."

"Helping isn't sacrificing yourself."

"Sometimes it is. Did you notice she was pregnant?" Bexley looked up to see his eyes widen as he shook his head. "I just—I couldn't let him take her. I knew if I asked, he would trade. So I did." She clenched her jaw as she pushed her hair back, eyes downward and uninterested in a lecture.

His finger tapped on her knee. She smirked and stopped his finger, then he grabbed her hand up at once.

"Bexley, look at me."

She found his cobalt blue eyes staring at her.

"What you did, was amazing. I've never seen anyone do that."

"I don't believe that."

He frowned, looking like she had just punched the wind out of him.

"You were in the military. I have a hard time believing you've never seen sacrifice."

"It's not the same."

"Why not?"

"Do you have to argue every point?" His tone dropped as he shook his head.

She shrugged. "I just don't see how it's different," she mumbled.

As she started to pull away, he used both hands to surround

hers. His large hands sandwiched hers and she could no longer see anything but her small wrist protruding from his palms.

"I'm sorry for getting upset, but you tend to argue."

"Maybe you just bring it out in me." She chuckled.

"I can live with that."

She stilled and licked her lips, her face heating up.

"In any case, it was amazing. But I'd appreciate it if you could refrain from doing that again anytime soon. At least until you heal up."

"Then, I guess you better catch the guy who took me." She looked up to see a grin on his face.

"Yes, ma'am." He winked and stood. "Consider me on the job."

"Good to know," she murmured with a grin.

He gave her another wink before closing the door as he left.

As Evan descended the staircase, he had a smile on his face. It felt good to have her here where he could protect her. Well, where the team could protect her. And it was better than whatever that Tennison guy could offer.

"Are you smiling?" Jeff's voice rang out as he looked up to see everyone standing at the kitchen island staring at him.

"He is. Wow. Didn't think I'd see the day." Sergio leaned into the island.

He dropped the smile as he made it to the kitchen. "Very funny."

"Told you, vexing." Haiden stared him down.

"What?" Jeff looked between him and Haiden, puzzled.

"Nothing. But I do want to make a point in case someone else didn't know. Bexley isn't big on physical contact. If you have to lead her, let her know first."

Grabbing a plate, Evan filled it and followed everyone to the couch.

Fighter

"Have you asked her about the conversation? Didn't she mention Arlo calling?"

Evan nodded to Buck as he finished his bite. "Yeah, when she called, she mentioned it. But I haven't had a chance to talk to her. She's pretty worn out."

"Understandable. First yesterday's drama, now the guy's trashing her house with her in it. It's like the worst stalker movie ever," Danica mumbled. "At least she can rest here."

Evan nodded, no longer hungry. Yeah, she was here, and that was what he wanted. But he hadn't even thought about that angle. She had to be reeling from the whole ordeal.

"Arlo was parked in a blue or black sedan across from Bexley's house. There isn't a house there, just an empty lot. The neighbors the police talked to had become curious." Jeff picked up his burger.

"We even have a positive ID from one man that was walking his dog. He noticed a strange man walking from Bex's house and got a good look."

Evan nodded to Sergio, then took a drink of his coke. "The message—why does he suddenly want to find her? She doesn't know anything we don't already have on him."

Jeff shrugged. "I don't know. This new plan could be enough to catch him. We still don't have his actual target yet, and that means we're left grasping at straws trying to catch up. If we know he's after her, he might make a mistake."

"Do you think he's using her as a distraction? I mean, to keep us tracking her instead of figuring out what he's actually doing here?" Evan found the whole thing odd.

Buck shrugged. "Could be. I'm still waiting on some things from Homeland about his financials. That should lead us to who's funding him, and then we'll be able to determine what the target is." Buck pulled a fry from his plate as he spoke, then shoved it in his mouth.

"She gonna eat?"

Evan looked up at Haiden's comment and shrugged. "I'm gonna let her rest."

"Sounds good. But I do want to discuss her conversation with Arlo. Plus, I've got to get her permission to trace her phone. See if we can figure out where the call came from." Buck wiped his mouth. "Do we have any new information?"

"After digging into the files Homeland's given us access to, there's not much about where he's been. He's originally from Syria, but that doesn't mean that's where he lives. I've not been able to link a ship coming in recently from that area." Sergio paused to take a drink.

Jeff leaned back on the couch. "And we're missing three men according to the prints. The warehouse had three distinct prints that don't match the men in the morgue. Although, I doubt they know anything about Arlo and his actual plan."

Evan frowned. "Why not?"

"Arlo is a sociopath who believes everyone is out to get him. I'm certain he didn't reveal anything more than breaching the bank. But this new turn with Bexley, it's odd."

"Maybe he is insane," Evan murmured.

Jeff huffed. "There's got to be more to it."

"The bank."

Evan looked up at Danica's wide eyes. "What about it?"

"I know it might be a nightmare to do, but what about the bank? Are there any accounts there he could be looking for? Any connections?"

Buck huffed as he sat down his plate. "You're right, that is a nightmare. Okay, I'll see what I can do discreetly. That's a good idea, Dani." Buck pulled out his phone and started texting.

Danica's phone rang, and she groaned. "Hang on," she muttered as she stood and rushed from the room.

Buck's eyes cut to Danica for a moment, then went back to texting.

"What did he mean by next time? Did he really think threatening her wouldn't put her in some kind of protection?"

Sergio set down his napkin. "Are we sure there isn't more with Bexley than what we know?"

"You think she's involved?" Evan set a glare on Sergio.

Sergio shrugged and leaned in on his knees. "I looked into her and that firm she used to work with. She's been out of the country several times, but never to Syria. I can see if her overseas visits ever link up to Arlo. At least what information I have on his movements."

"Go ahead and look at it. We don't have anything else to focus on." Buck nodded.

Clenching his jaw, Evan kept his comments to himself. They didn't see Arlo yank Bexley around, see her reaction to the attack at the bookstore.

"Ev."

His eyes locked on Haiden.

"Easy."

Following Haiden's gaze, he noticed his hand fisted. Releasing it, he blew out a breath. He needed to find a way to shift his focus.

17

After throwing away the rest of his dinner, Evan sat down on the couch.

Danica descended the steps. "I think Bexley's up. I hear the hairdryer." She turned and headed down the hallway.

"I'll see if she's ready to come down." Jeff headed up the staircase, Evan watching.

"What's that look for, Ev?" Sergio's grin irked Evan.

"What're you talking about?"

"Please. You're hung up on her. I don't blame you. She's got it all—looks and skills."

"You're married," Evan said flatly.

"Yep, but none of these other guys are." Sergio winked.

Evan's hands fisted at his sides.

"Cool it, man. We all know, we can see it already." Sergio's chuckle echoed.

"See what?" Evan jaw ached from gritting his teeth.

"She's yours."

Evan's gaze shifted to Buck, who had a smirk on his face too.

"Actually, no, she's not."

"Vexing." Haiden's eyebrow shot up.

Evan groaned. "Look …"

"She'll be down in a minute." Jeff's face and neck shone red as he took a seat at the island.

Evan huffed. "Let's just get back to the case."

"Did you find out about any deposits?" Buck's gaze centered on Evan.

"No, no deposits." Evan sighed with relief as the focus shifted. "According to the bank manager, they have routine pickups alternating days. Nothing big going down."

"And your research into her, anything there?"

"I did some digging on Reggie White. She's the friend at Bexley's home when I showed up. Apparently, they worked at the same firm."

"I asked you to look into *Bexley*, not her friends," Buck muttered.

"Look, she's a link to the bigger picture, right? Maybe I can find out why she was let go and what kind of worker she is."

Sergio snorted. "From a friend? You know this woman will just stick up for Bexley."

Evan shrugged. "She might. But she also might tell me why Bexley no longer works there."

"Did you ever think to ask her?"

"I figure she'd offer it up, Jeff, if it wasn't a big deal," Evan muttered. "She's not mentioned it, so I think there might be more to it."

"So, what do you think so far?"

With a sigh, Evan leaned up on his knees, Buck's stern gaze fixed on him. "She's well trained in *protective* services. She even renewed her license last week even though she's no longer doing that job."

Buck nodded. "I talked with her immediate boss. She was lead. Has been in charge of their protection team for almost two years. Her boss was disappointed to lose her."

"Then why did she leave?"

Buck shrugged at Evan's question. "He just said it wasn't his call. Came from much higher up the food chain."

"Well, that brings up other questions." Jeff stood from the island and perched on the couch's arm. "If she was that dedicated to her career, that well-trained and well-respected by her boss, what happened to convince the higher-ups to let her go?"

BEXLEY THREW her towel into the hamper in the bathroom.

"That was a complete embarrassment," she muttered.

Jeff's abrupt intrusion as she was standing in just a towel made her face heat. He obviously thought she said to come in instead of hang on. Not the best first impression with a group of men who are supposed to be protecting her. Although she'd already embarrassed herself in front of Jeff once ...

Another knock on the door made her jump.

Get a grip, Bex.

"Bexley, it's me. Buck wants a word." Evan's voice echoed through the door.

She pulled her hair through her fingers and smoothed it down, trying to ease those ever-present self-conscious feelings. She pulled on her shoes and answered the door to see Evan leaning against the wall.

"You okay?" He narrowed his eyes.

"Yeah, just sore."

"Got your phone?"

She turned and pulled it from the charger.

"Let's go." He took off down the stairwell before she could even get back to the door.

So, he suddenly wanted nothing to do with her? What was with all the flirting earlier? Well, maybe he wasn't really flirting.

Taking a breath, she headed down the hallway. When it came to her job, she was good. All business. But her personal life? That was another story. Her history of dating losers would support that fact.

Slowly descending the staircase, she paused and waited for the dizziness to ease. As she looked up, Jeff approached her on the steps.

"Ignore his attitude. He's embarrassed," Jeff lowered his voice and offered his arm for assistance.

She took it, helping to steady herself down the steps. "I'm really sorry you didn't hear me earlier." Not knowing how to bring up such an embarrassing moment, she made a face.

"No, it's my fault. I should've waited for you to open the door. Don't worry, I didn't say anything." He whispered the last part, and she smiled as they reached the landing.

"Have a seat, Miss Bowers."

She nodded as Jeff walked to the island, and she took a seat on the couch.

"Call me Bexley or Bex." She let out a breath as she gripped her side. "What ... I mean, what do you need to know?"

"You spoke with your attacker earlier. What did he say?"

Leaning back, she eased her legs up in the seat with her. "He said he studied my past and that we were connected. His parents were killed when he was young as well."

Buck didn't seem the least bit surprised then she remembered Jeff mentioning doing their homework on her. Great.

"What else?"

Her focus went back to Buck. "Just that and the fact he wanted to take me up on the offer to help him."

"Help him do what?" Evan walked up behind Buck.

She shrugged. "I have no idea. I told him that offer was no longer on the table and hung up."

"So, he was trying to say you two were connected?" Jeff crossed his arms as he stood in front of her.

"Yes. Why?"

"I think we found our reasoning."

"Reasoning? Reasoning for what?" She furrowed her brow at

Jeff, who just straightened and glanced at Evan. "What's going on?" She looked to Evan, who simply walked away.

"There was a message at your house. It said, 'until next time.'" Buck watched her intently.

"What?" She swallowed her anger. "You think that because I got away, he wants to come after me? That seems a little extreme. I mean, I'm sure he has something much more pressing than dealing with me, right? He has other plans, I heard him say that." She looked between the men around her, hearing the fear build in her own voice.

Jeff shrugged. "He's trying to make a connection with you, get you on his terms. Whatever help he wants from you, he's going to make sure he gets it."

She took a deep breath. "Okay, so now what? I thought you knew where he was. Just go get him."

"It's not that easy. While we know who he is, we can't produce him. He's in hiding." Buck shook his head. "Homeland is working on his contacts and the money trail, though. It's just a matter of time."

The seriousness of the situation hammered into her.

"So, I'm genuinely a target now?" She tried to take a few breaths to ease the pounding of her heart.

"Yes. We'll work with you as much as we can, but I'm afraid if the FBI or Homeland want to step in, they might want to put you in protective custody." Buck clenched his jaw as hers fell open.

"I thought I was already in protective custody?" She tore her stare from Buck and put it on Evan. "That's what you said, right? If I chose to stay here—"

"We're not that kind of agency." Evan frowned, raking his hand back and forth through his hair. "We're a response team. If something else comes up here locally, we could get called in and might not be able to leave someone behind to protect you."

"Don't worry. I'm going to do what I can to keep you here and keep you safe. We'll find him and get this cinched up, okay?"

Buck took her attention. "I need your phone. I've got a friend who can clone this one so you'll have it. He'll get the GPS disconnected too. I want to trace that call Arlo made, figure out where he was calling from."

"Arlo? That's his name?"

Buck nodded. "Sound familiar? Arlo Androssier."

She frowned, shaking her head. "No, not familiar at all," she murmured.

"Your phone?" Buck held out his hand.

"Sure, whatever you need." She handed it over and sat back, completely dumbfounded and shocked by the message left at her home.

This Arlo guy was actually coming after her, and she had no idea why.

A WOMAN about Bexley's height with short black hair sat down on the ottoman in front of her.

"Danica Freeman, this is Bexley Bowers." Jeff introduced them.

"Great to finally meet you. Officially, that is." Danica flashed a grin.

"Come on, Bexley. You need to eat."

Her gaze fell to the plate filled with a burger and fries Jeff handed her.

"Thanks," she mumbled.

"Well, someone had to be a gentleman around here."

The sarcastic tone made her smirk as she watched Jeff take his time walking past Evan. Evan, however, looked like he was ready to take a swing. His glare shifted to her for a second.

"Gentleman, huh?" Danica winked in Evan's direction.

He huffed and walked off.

"So, you settled in?" Danica leaned in on her knees, clutching a phone.

Fighter

"I guess as good as I'll ever be."

Danica chuckled. "Yeah, well, it's a home away from home. It took me some time to get used to it too. It's not so much the room, it's the company," she whispered with a chuckle as groans echoed all around her.

"Are you saying you don't like living with us most of the year?" Jeff held his hand to his chest with a pout.

"Hey, as long as I have my own room and bathroom where I can escape from you people, I'm good."

Bexley listened intently to the conversation that flowed around her as the others from the team trickled in to sit on the couch. Danica was obviously the center of attention, talkative and friendly, managing to include everyone in the conversation. Her big brown eyes held each one as she spoke, offering sarcastic commentary and occasionally rolling her eyes at their remarks.

Haiden, the man who had trailed them at the mall, sat down at the end of the couch, his head down and focused on his phone. He didn't really say much but chimed in every once in a while with a short phrase or two.

He had a hat down low over his face, but she could see the clean cut of his hair and a freshly shaven face with no shadow on his square jaw. Several inches taller than her five-five frame, his arms looked heavily muscled under his Henley.

Loud laughter caught her attention. Sergio sat down on the recliner with a grin. He was a man with a sense of humor. His laughter carried through the large, open space, and she smiled. He was the same height as Haiden but much stouter, with jet black hair worn short and spiked.

Jeff sat down next to her, propping his leg up on the ottoman while he spoke. He appeared to have no problems being part of the group. She appreciated his kindness in Evan's absence.

Unfortunately, her mind and her eyes kept wandering back to the island and to Evan, who sat by himself, simply watching the animated group of people he worked with.

"Come on, Dane, let's go over this Arlo thing again."

"Don't call me that, Jeff. You know I hate that." Danica frowned as she stood and followed him to the kitchen.

"Everyone here has a nickname, you know that."

"Really? What are they?" She smiled as Jeff's face dropped a moment.

"Oh, well—"

"Mine is Funny Man, obviously." Sergio grinned, and she chuckled. "Haiden's is the Quiet Man. It's an old show or something, but it fits him. Danica is Dane, Jeff is the Albino."

She laughed out loud and Jeff's face turned red.

"Buck is the Hunter, and Evan is the Fire Master."

Bexley covered her mouth to try and hide her amusement but ended up chuckling pretty loudly anyway as Evan shook his head. "Those are some interesting nicknames."

"Yeah, interesting." Evan scoffed as he walked off.

Everyone filtered from the room, leaving her sitting on the couch, trying to find a way to make herself eat. Taking a breath, she set the plate down on the ottoman, the surge of loneliness and fear coming over her again.

"What are you trying to do to me, God?" she muttered under her breath as she wiped her face.

God seemed to think she needed to be here for some reason, so what was her purpose? Why did he save her?

Shaking her head, she let out a deep breath. It was official—she was the target of a madman.

18

Arlo paced the small room, his thoughts cluttering and frustration building.

He'd lost her. Just when he thought he'd have a way to get to her once his team arrived, she was gone.

In such a large town, he had no idea someone would show up so fast to her home. He had anticipated having more than enough time to throw the gas bomb into the room, grab her over his shoulder and take off.

But that large man had arrived within minutes and put her in an SUV. Arlo had tailed them perfectly until they hit yet another highway system. Between the darkness and traffic, they had escaped.

Americans always did well at making people disappear, but they had no idea what he was capable of.

Gritting his teeth, he sat down at the computer, studying the plans for the new bank. It was larger, in a busy part of the city, and with three guards to combat. Not only did he need another large group to take on the security, but men who would obey without questions.

Bexley. She would have to be his key if this new plan didn't work out. Either way, she was a loose end.

His hands fisted. His revenge was so close, within his grasp, and it slipped away each time. He'd waited long enough.

"Next time, I will get what's mine."

"He's a narcissistic, paranoid psycho. I just don't see why he's after Bexley." Jeff leaned against the door.

"She said he was accepting her help. So, what could Bexley help him with?" Evan stood at Buck's desk as they went over the situation with Arlo.

"It's all connected to the bank," Buck mumbled. "What access could he have from that bank branch that he wouldn't have anywhere else?"

Jeff straightened. "That bank would have access to probably all other branches and systems. But being a small office in the mall, it might not have the manpower and security."

"Maybe not an actual security guard, but it would have security systems in place, just like anywhere else." Danica said. "Just because there's not a physical presence doesn't mean the online security isn't the same."

"Does that bank have international connections?" Buck asked.

Surfing through her phone, Danica pulled up the bank's profile. "Yeah, looks like it has an international presence."

"Homeland said that Arlo was able to access information from their system. Do we know exactly what was accessed?"

Buck shook his head at Jeff's question. "Nope, still waiting on Homeland for that."

Evan let out a huff. "So, the question remains, why Bexley?"

As they sat in silence, Buck stroked the stubble on his chin, staring at the wall.

"Why are we doing this research, Buck? This is Homeland's turf or, at the very least, the FBI. Why are we looking into this so hard?" Danica leaned back, turning her phone over on her knee.

Buck cut his eyes to her for a moment. "You don't like figuring this out?"

She shrugged. "Is this a training exercise?"

"No, not a training exercise." Buck leaned on the desk. "This is a chance for all of you to see into the mind of the bad guy. We deal in negotiations with these kinds of people. What is his motivation for being here? Why is he suddenly after Bexley? According to Sergio's research, we know she's not been in Syria or any area at the same time Arlo was assumed to be there, so there's no way she's the reason he's in the U.S."

"That's why going after Bexley doesn't make sense. She can't help him do anything he and his men can't do," Evan mumbled.

"I still think Arlo has a plan for her." Jeff sat down on the couch. "He's got to be in control of everything around him. His paranoia won't allow anyone near him he can't control."

"Do you think he'll come after her here?" Danica's eyes went wide.

Evan shook his head. "Our security is tight, and we're not a place you can just pull up online."

"Not unless he has a whole team with him like last time," Jeff mumbled.

Danica nodded. "I'm beat. See you guys in the morning."

As Danica left, Jeff let out a sigh.

"What's up?" Evan asked.

"Something's going on with Danica." Jeff's eyes cut to Buck. "She say anything to you?"

"Just had a bad day yesterday. Things are good now."

Obviously, there was more going on, but it was odd that Jeff and Buck both seemed to share the same concern. Although Evan knew Buck from his previous job, he had no idea how Jeff and Danica fit into the picture with Buck.

What was he missing here?

"Hey, I'm glad you're still up."

Bexley looked up as Danica came in, kicking off her shoes and sitting on her bed.

"Yeah, well, I've napped a lot today." Bexley sat down her phone and sat up with a grimace.

"That's understandable, you've had a busy few days. You need help with something?"

Bexley shook her head as she adjusted her position. "No, I'm just uncomfortable."

"Give it some time, things will get better."

"Yeah," Bexley mumbled. "So, tell me about you. How long have you worked with this group?"

"Since Buck started it, about two years ago." Danica grinned as she leaned back against the wall. "Buck is friends with the mayor and the chief of police. They had mentioned needing more help with response times. Dallas is a big area, and even with the SWAT team and the police, they were short when it came to the northeast areas. So, Buck looked into it and found a way to get funding. He brought Jeff on board, and as soon as they had the money aside to get the planning going, I joined in. We do a gala every year to try and raise money."

"There's a gala?" Bexley smirked.

Danica chuckled. "Oh yeah. Buck has a friend that puts it on every year for us. I think it's a tax write-off for her. Anyway, it's one of the ways we stay in business. We get a little state help, but most of our salaries come from private donors and investors. So, every year we get dressed up and have a party."

"I cannot see Evan in a tux, mingling with people!" Bexley let out a laugh.

Danica smiled. "That's a pretty funny picture. I have a feeling he's going to be giving Buck a hard time about it. I'm not even sure he knew about it until last week when Buck brought it up. We do it right before Thanksgiving."

"So, he hasn't been to one yet?"

"No."

"Do you have your dress picked out?"

Danica scoffed. "I'm more of a wait-till-the-last-minute kind of girl."

"Well, if you need some help or an honest opinion, I'll be available. At least, I hope I'll be available then."

"I know you will. With all the people looking for Arlo, we'll find him. Thanks for the offer. I don't have anyone here I can take with me. Maybe you would want to go to the gala too?"

Bexley could feel her face heating. "No, I don't—I mean, I'm not good at that kind of stuff."

"Wouldn't it be worth it to see Evan all dressed up? He might even wear his uniform."

Bexley grinned. "Yeah, that might be worth it, but it would be just fanning the flames to something completely pointless."

Danica chuckled. "You never know. Besides, I have a feeling you're just the person to push through his tough exterior."

"I don't know about that," Bex muttered as she leaned her head back against the wall.

"I saw his reaction to you being taken. He's definitely got something going on."

Bexley shook her head. "No, nothing's going on, trust me. I think that was more the heat of the moment. He's an action guy, reacting to the danger and fixing the problem. Worked with a lot of that kind in my day."

Danica furrowed her brow. "Well, they all have their hangups. I mean, look at Haiden. He's so quiet and stern one minute, and then next thing you know, he has something profound to say."

"Yeah, he is quiet." Bexley nodded, noticing the flush on Danica's cheeks.

"I'll let you get some rest, okay?"

"Thanks, I just ... I'm a little out of it, I guess," Bexley murmured.

"Let me know if you need anything."

Bexley nodded as the overhead light went out, leaving her sitting on her bed in the glow of her cell phone. Reactionary, that definitely described Evan. But the way he'd helped her, been there for her without asking anything in return, it had meant something.

At least, it did to her.

EVAN MULLED the comments floating through the closed door to Bexley and Danica's room. Although the reminder about the gala made him want to retreat to his room, hearing Bexley's comment about fanning the flames made him wonder.

So, was she with that Tennison guy?

Danica stepped from the room, closing the door behind her with a frown.

"What? I was just checking on Bexley." His brows furrowed.

She motioned to the back of the hallway, and he followed. She turned and glared up at him.

"Look, I have no idea what's going on, but you need to either step up or step back."

"Excuse me?" He crossed his arms.

"I saw your reaction to her leaving with Arlo and then after you secured her in that ambulance. If you don't want to act on it, fine. But just remember, she can leave when she wants to. Don't give her a reason to want to get away from here."

"I'm not doing or saying anything that would confuse her. Besides, pretty sure she already has a boyfriend."

Danica's eyebrow arched. "Oh?" She gazed down the hallway past him. "Then I guess you don't have a reason to step up, do you?" He frowned at the wink she gave him before heading down the back staircase.

Groaning, Evan headed back to the computer and sat down with a huff.

"You like to eavesdrop?" Haiden stared from under his hat.

"I wasn't eavesdropping. I was going to ask Bexley if she needed anything. But Danica had her covered." Evan cleared his throat and ignored the glare. "What?" He hoped his irritated tone was enough to stave Haiden off.

"What were you and Danica talking about?" Haiden's voice dropped.

"None of your business." Evan turned back to the computer.

Step up or step back.

Stepping up wasn't really his thing, and if Bexley was in a relationship with that guy, there would be no use in stepping up anyway. But she didn't act all that interested in Tennison staying and the way she pulled out of his reach ...

"I'm going to work out." He slammed the keyboard and stood, stomping to the stairwell.

19

Bexley stood at the back window, staring at the darkened sky.

After trying to sleep, her mind got the better of her, and she decided to walk the hallway to get out her nervous energy.

Danica said she and Jeff would be working in the office on the first floor if Bex needed anything, and everyone else was either in their rooms or gone. Here she could stand alone, hide away from everyone and their questions.

Her buzzing phone pulled her from gazing out the window.

"Hello?" she murmured.

"Bex?"

Her breath stalled in her throat at the sound of Tennison's voice.

"Hello? Did I lose you?"

"Um, no." She forced out a breath. "Why're you calling?"

"Where are you? I went by your house, and there was police tape out front. What's going on?"

"Nothing I can discuss," she mumbled.

"It's obvious you need some *professional* help. I want to help and I want to talk."

She sighed. "Tennison, I don't have anything I want to talk about with you."

"Just because we broke up doesn't mean I don't still care about you."

"And my job?"

He huffed. "That was my father's doing. You know how he is."

"Then why didn't you stop him?"

"I tried. But he was set on making distance. He's the one who implemented that rule about in-house dating."

Leaning her head in her hand, she closed her eyes. "I can't talk right now."

"I want you safe. I'm still not entirely sure why you had to leave in the first place."

"You know why," she muttered.

The bruises on her arms, the anger that filled his features every time something didn't go his way. Tennison not only had a bad temper but was controlling, demanding ...

"No, actually, I don't. You never told me why."

"Tenn, you ... you have anger issues."

"I told you I'm working on that. Bexley, I love you. I think you should come home where I can protect you."

"I—" She paced the hallway, attempting to find a train of thought that didn't involve being back in Tennison's arms. "I left because of you and the fact that things were getting ... heated."

"I never, ever hit you. I never would."

"The fact you have to voice that is evidence you knew what you were doing," she whispered.

"I thought you loved me too. Or was that a lie?"

"I did. But I can't go back. Not now."

After God giving her a second chance at a new life, connecting with Tennison would be a disaster. The way he looked at her, spoke to her, held her, it all made her feel so wanted and loved. But when it was bad ...

"Tell me what happened. Why not now?"

Fighter

Leaning a shoulder against the wall, she stared at her reflection in the window. "I just can't. What we were doing, living together and all the fighting, it wasn't right."

Silence stretched a moment.

"Bex, I know I should've told you sooner, but I wanted to start talking about our future."

She straightened. "What?"

"I had already made plans to ask you to marry me. We did talk about that, remember?"

"We had only been dating a few months when you brought that up. I thought you were joking," she whispered, unable to get her voice to work.

"I wasn't. I love you, and that's not going to change. I just want to know if you can still love me. What if you come to therapy with me?"

Unable to speak, she forced in a breath. "Tenn, I'm glad ... I'm glad you're getting help. But I have to go."

His sigh echoed over the line. "Bexley, call if you need anything. I mean it, I love you."

Dumbfounded, she shook her head. "I'll talk to you later. Bye."

Hanging up, she shoved the phone in her back pocket.

Marriage? Was he serious about marriage? Her personal life had been a disaster as long as she could remember. Finding herself alone far too often, she turned to whoever would offer her comfort. Tennison had been the one man she thought would turn into something more. But his anger shocked her once they were living together.

Closing her eyes, she leaned back against the wall. Embarrassed at where her life ended up, she was so thankful God thought her important enough to save. Now if she could find a way to get her life back together, allow God to make the decisions instead of falling for whatever handsome man stood in front of her.

It was pointless to daydream about a man she'd walked away

from, especially when she feared his anger would get the best of him. Then there was Evan ...

"Couldn't sleep?"

Stifling a scream, Bexley covered her mouth.

"Bexley?" Evan stood there, reaching out but refraining from touching her.

"What're you doing up here?" She shook out her fisted hand.

"I was headed to the computers. What're *you* doing?"

The smell of shampoo and soap drifted around him, his messy hair still damp and those cobalt eyes set on her.

"Bexley?"

"Just couldn't sleep," she mumbled as she retreated to the stairwell.

Before she reached the landing, dizziness overwhelmed her as a sharp pain pushed into her back, a groan coming through her lips.

"Hey, what's wrong?"

"I ... I can't breathe." She gripped her side, the pain slicing through the muscles.

The sound of wheels on the wood floor echoed. "Sit." He lowered her to a chair, and she closed her eyes. "Bex, look at me." He tapped her knee, and she struggled to focus. "Slow down, you're going to hyperventilate. Slow breaths."

"I ... I just ... can't take in a breath."

"Stop trying to talk." He pushed his fingers through hers.

She closed her eyes and leaned forward as Evan knelt in front of her, pulling her to him. Resting her head against his shoulder, her breathing settled. She gripped his shoulder as she twisted every now and then, trying to ease the muscles in her side and back.

"Let me take a look."

She shook her head as she leaned back.

"I'm a professional, okay? I just want to see how bad it is."

His hand steadied her elbow as she stood. Holding the shirt

tightly in front with her injured right arm, she let him pull it up on the side.

"Wow, that looks bad."

"Professional, huh?" she muttered.

"Sorry." He flashed a smile. "We need to get you some ice."

"I just ... I've had injuries before, but all this," she whispered as she closed her eyes and tried to breathe through the shooting pain. "Between my hand and my side, then I keep getting dizzy ..."

"I'm sorry, Bex." He stepped closer as she gripped his upper arms, her head leaning into his chest.

His arms gently wrapped around to her back as his fingers played with the ends of her hair. She smiled. Attempting to ignore the feeling of his muscled arms under her hands, she tried to relax. The motion of circles he rubbed into her back lulled her.

Evan's throat cleared. "Um, maybe you should sit down. I need to get you that ice," he mumbled.

"Yeah." She nodded, but neither let go.

She enjoyed being here, being held. And it seemed God put Evan here to help her, give her support as she dealt with the fallout of the past few days. But if God sent Evan, why was Tennison showing up and offering everything she'd ever wanted?

Stepping back, she kept her gaze down as she headed to the stairs. Taking hold of the rail, she eased herself down the steps.

"You need to take it easy."

"It's not like I'm running a marathon," she muttered. "I've sat around all day. My mind is just awake with everything going on." She headed for the couch and paused.

Frowning at her need to sit and the fact she could barely bend over, she closed her eyes a moment.

"Come on." He pulled at her arm, and she yanked away, turning as her hand fisted.

His jaw set as something washed over him, his eyes flashing worry instead of anger. "Look, I'm not going to sit here and pretend that reaction is involuntary. I've seen that more than once, and now I think I know. You should talk to someone."

"None of your business, Evan," she murmured. "Next time, don't grab me when my eyes are closed."

She worked to even her tone, but between exhaustion and pain, she couldn't keep from just sounding weepy.

"Good to know. And it's not my business, but I'm not going to pretend I don't have an idea. I won't react to it anymore, look at you like you should know better. But you need to get it out. Just know I'm here if you want to talk." He offered a hand, and she took it as she sat down.

Grabbing a pillow, she leaned her forehead into it, hiding her face as she tried to keep from crying. She never used to react like that. But after living with Tennison for six months and now all this …

Evan sat down next to her, tapping her knee like before. "I'm sorry."

His arm went around her shoulders, prodding her closer. She leaned into him, holding up her sore hand as she tried to ease her body. Eyes closed, she prayed.

Lord, please take away this pain. I don't know how to handle all this, and then Tennison talking about love and marriage? I'm so weak right now. Please, God, please give me strength.

EVAN WAITED for her sobs to ease and her breaths to even out.

"Let me get you some ice."

"I can get it." She sat up.

He gently took hold of her elbow.

"What? I can get the ice. I wanted a drink too," her hoarse voice whispered.

"I'll get it. What do you want?"

"I don't like to be waited on. I can move."

"Just tell me what you want."

"Whatever you have."

He nodded and stood, going to the kitchen, and returning with a bag of ice and a Coke.

Handing her the Coke, he sat the ice on her side then grabbed a blanket. After covering her up, he sat down on the ottoman in front of her.

"Let's talk, get your mind off it."

"I can't. I can't even think right now. Just ... tell me about the people you work with."

"Why?"

She wiped her face, straining to move around as a grimace covered her features. He clasped his hands to keep from reaching out.

"Everyone knows about me, give me some information on everyone else. Do you each have your own job or what?"

She finally settled and looked up. Her bright green eyes, rimmed in red, searched his.

"Not really. We all have different backgrounds that give us a little more experience in different areas." He narrowed his eyes, wondering just where this line of questioning could go. "Just like the other day, I'm not the only one that can defuse a bomb, but I have more training."

"From the Navy?"

And there it was.

"I don't like to talk about it."

"Why not?" She forced a grin, and he couldn't help but smile back.

"Not gonna happen." He chuckled at her frown, finding it equally amusing.

"Fine, tell me about everyone else."

He swallowed and took a breath. "Haiden is a former Ranger. He's our weapons expert, although we all have training there. Jeff is a former Homeland agent. His training provides us with the ability to arrest if needed, although we usually leave that up to the other agencies. He also worked a stint with ICE."

She took several sips of her coke, then leaned back.

"Danica is former ATF, Sergio worked as a SWAT team member before going back to the PD, then here. He can do anything with computers."

"How did you end up here?" Her soft voice drew him in.

Curled up in the blanket, lying on her right side, it took a lot of heavenly intervention to keep from sitting down next to her and wrapping her up.

She was right—he had protective instincts that helped him in his job. But he had never really had them with anyone on a personal level—at least, not with a woman. His former teammates, yeah, but with her, he felt himself tensing all the time as he watched her struggle with her injuries, wanting to help.

"Evan?"

He grinned at the fact she said his name, his focus finally shifting back to her. "Buck hired me about six months ago."

He worried she would pry, but her gaze went to her hands as she held her Coke.

The stitched-up cut to her scalp made his jaw clench. It sat just below her hairline and was probably the reason she was dizzy so often. The large brace on her hand, the deep bruise on her side, it was all because he let her take the hits in the bookstore. It should've been him.

"I think ... I think I need to go back to bed," she whispered.

He could hear the tears below the surface. Taking the glass from her hand, he helped her stand. A heavy murmur escaped her lips, and she once more closed her eyes.

"Let me carry you, okay? It's not a big deal, no one will know."

"I don't want to be carried."

Those bright eyes shone through the dark circles, proving that fire was still there despite her injuries.

Nodding, he guided her past the couch to the stairs, taking most of her weight.

"Bex, just up the stairs, okay?"

She finally nodded, taking a ragged breath. Stepping to her uninjured side, he pulled her up in his arms as she curled to his chest. He took the stairs easily.

"I'm good now."

Her gentle voice made the hair stand up on his neck as he kept going. Walking into her room, he sat her down gently next to her bed. A tug on his shirt made him look down to see her holding on, her eyes closed as she worked her breathing.

"Bex?"

"Yeah, just give me a minute," she whispered.

Rubbing her arms up and down, he did what he could to keep his hands busy. The pull on his shirt was already bad enough. He half expected something more when he looked down. Maybe he just hoped for something more.

"Okay, I think I'm good."

"Text me if you need something," he murmured, her eyes focused on his chest as she nodded.

Trying to swallow the lump in his throat, he made himself leave the room.

Closing the door behind him, he let out a breath. He had to stop finding his way in that room with her. Being alone made one too many things pop into his mind. This attraction was really getting to him.

"Get a grip," he muttered.

Focus on work, you need this work.

She could easily be with that Tennison guy or maybe getting back together with him. But if Evan saw that guy grab her arm ever again ... Taking a breath, he sat down in front of the computer, hoping to find some focus in his work.

Attraction he could handle, he could manage. But ever since he met Bexley Bowers, something else was prying into his brain and his heart, something he couldn't explain.

"God, what're you doing to me?" he whispered.

20

Evan sat on his bed, Bible in hand, and stared blankly at the wall.

There was no focusing this morning, nothing he could do to make his mind ease. Danica's comment to step up or step back rattled in his brain.

How could he possibly be the man God wanted of him and be so ... stubborn?

Three years, it had been three years since he was in any kind of situation with a woman. After that disaster and starting Bible study on the base with a few of the guys, he had met Buck.

That study etched into his brain, Colossians 3:17. "And whatever you do, in word or in deed, do everything in the name of the Lord Jesus, giving thanks to God the Father through him."

He wasn't exactly living the way God wanted, he imagined, but he was trying. These past three years had hit him hard, and he was still struggling to deal. In fact, if Buck hadn't hunted him down after his discharge, he imagined his life would be much worse, much more detrimental.

The explosion that effectively ended his career, the anger and rage he had held on to, and the way he stepped away from his own family, it was a disaster of a life he had created for himself.

This job had centered him, reminded him that he was here for a purpose. And having Buck and other believers around him helped remind him who he was in Christ. Although he struggled to open up to his teammates, he was there and trying.

"God, give me some peace."

He'd tried to pray—pray for God's guidance, Arlo's apprehension, and for Bexley. She was dealing with a lot more than she was willing to open up about, and he hated that she was closing herself off.

"Heal her Lord, mind and body. Give me the right words at the right time."

IN THE EARLY MORNING, Bexley stood in the bathroom, brushing out her hair as the sound of a knock paused her mid-stroke.

Knowing it was probably Evan, she set the brush down and took a deep breath. Last night he came to her aid, helping her, carrying her, and making her feel way more than she needed to about him. She was already trying to forget about Tennison and his profession of love and marriage. Having Evan be so amazing was just frustrating. Not that it meant anything to him, he was just reacting. Probably.

"Hey." Evan stood there, looking much too handsome and ready for action in a black tactical vest.

"Can I help you?"

He smirked. "Sergio is staying here, but the rest of us are headed out to check on a lead."

"Okay, good luck. I hope you get him."

"Me too." His eyes narrowed. "You feeling okay?"

"Just fine."

"There's that word again."

"Really, I'm doing well, just a little sore."

His arms crossed, those cobalt blues stared down at her, making her heart kick up a notch. But she needed to make distance. Obviously, she wasn't the best judge of character when it came to men. Her thoughts went to Tennison, and her jaw clenched.

"You never mentioned that phone call last night."

Heat filled her face and she was helpless to stop it. "It was a —a personal call. Trust me, if it had been Arlo, I would've let you know."

He shoved his hands into his pockets. "Want to talk about it?"

"Nothing to talk about."

His eyes narrowed. "That Tennison guy, he seemed ... protective about you being home alone."

"As I recall, so did you." She crossed her arms. "I used to work with him. But I'm sure you already knew that."

"I did." His head tilted. "Why don't you work there anymore?"

Working her jaw, she eased the pounding of her heart. "It was a personal situation. I made a bad decision and lost my job because of it." Shifting back and forth, she licked her lips. "I thought you had to go?"

"I can take a minute." He stepped closer, his gentle voice soothing. "I always have time to listen, Bexley. You just gotta talk."

"I don't have anything to say," she muttered.

After watching her for a moment, he finally nodded. "If you need anything, just text. Okay?"

"Okay. Thanks," she murmured.

He offered a smile then turned, closing the door behind him.

PACING THE ROOM, Arlo frowned at the small group of men ready for action. His broker back home said he'd send the best, but these men didn't look like much.

"You gonna tell us what the job is?"

He turned and glared at the bearded man. Large and muscled, the mercenary could probably crush him in no time. But Arlo was smarter.

"Do you want to be paid?"

"What?"

Arlo stepped in front of the man. "If you're getting paid, what is it to you to wait here until the plan is set?"

The man shrugged.

"Fine. I'll be ready to lay out the plan this afternoon."

The man stood, motioning to the others to leave. Once the room emptied, Arlo called his broker.

"Hello?"

"You've sent me fools!" he sneered. "These were the best you could find?"

"Sir, your reputation proceeds you. Those were the men who responded."

Pacing, Arlo cursed. "Increase the price. I want five more here tomorrow."

"Five? Tomorrow?"

"It's either five more men or your head." Arlo hung up and tossed the phone on the table.

The original plan would never work with only four men and himself. They needed a much larger team to get inside the bank.

"Bexley Bowers."

Her name rolled off his tongue. With the new team, his need for her assistance seemed unnecessary. But now, lacking numbers to take on high security at the bank, she might be the best bet. The busy bank, the security, the original plan would only work if he had three times the men ready for action.

"Time to redirect my efforts," he muttered as he sat down and mulled over a new plan.

It would work. It had to work.

He had waited long enough, and the information he needed sat there taunting him. Bexley Bowers could get that info for him quickly, or her loved ones would pay the price.

21

"Hey, Bex. I'm glad you called."

Bexley grinned as she leaned back against the wall on her bed, Reggie's voice coming through the line.

"It's good to hear your voice."

"Oh? What's going on? 'Cause I drove by your house early this morning on my way to work and I swear I saw some police tape on the porch."

Bexley grimaced.

"So, do you want to tell me what's going on, or do I need to trace your phone?"

"You can try, but I don't think it's going to work," she muttered.

"Come on, Bex."

She let out a sigh. "Okay, but don't freak out on me." Silence stretched. "The guy from the other day, he broke into my house."

"What guy? That hot Evan guy?"

"No, no, of course not. The guy who attacked me."

"What? Why didn't you call?"

"Evan and the team showed up, took care of everything."

"Tell me you're not in police custody."

She forced a chuckle. "No. Evan's team has an office. The security is tight. I've already done a few walk-throughs. Sensors on everything and coded and key card locks on the doors. With the security they have in place and the firepower they have locked up, it's practically a fortress."

"Bex, you're starting to worry me here. Why is this guy coming after you?"

"I wish I knew. There's no connection from work or anything like that. I would've remembered his name and face."

She shivered. That face, his dark eyes staring right through her, haunted her nightmares.

"I'll help. I've got lots of vacation time and I want in."

"Regg, look, they've got this place well stocked, and this team is competent. I wouldn't stay here if they weren't. I do appreciate the offer."

Reggie's deep sigh echoed.

"I promise, if something comes up I can't handle and we need more backup, you're my first call."

"Fine." Reggie's clipped answer made Bexley frown. "But there's something else going on. What is it?"

Of course Reggie would ferret out the one thing she didn't want to talk about.

"Is it about Hot Evan?"

Bexley chuckled. "No, nothing to talk about there."

"No offense, but I don't think you'd be able to tell."

Bexley frowned. "Thanks for that."

"I mean it. For some reason, you just look past things when it comes to men. Take Tennison, for instance. The guy has some issues, but he has this big fake smile. You got hooked, and that was that."

Bexley leaned her head back against the wall and closed her eyes. "He came by yesterday."

"Tennison? When?"

"Right after you left. Evan was on his way out, and then Tennison shows up, all concerned."

"What did Evan say?" Reggie asked.

Bexley's eyes popped open. "What do you mean?"

"I mean, Evan seemed far too interested in you to simply step back just because Tennison was there. Why else did he show up instead of calling to let you know what was going on?"

That was the second comment about Evan being interested. Was she that blind?

"Bex?" Reggie's voice rang out.

"Yeah, I'm here." Bexley cleared her throat. "He told Tennison I was safe and then asked him to leave, which he did."

"And then?"

"That's it, nothing else happened. Tennison did call me last night, mentioned a few things—"

"Don't do that." Reggie's terse voice made Bexley frown. "Tennison is trying to make up to you, don't let him. He's a jerk, and I know you know that."

"I never said I believed him or was going to get back together with him. I just couldn't believe he was so interested. He wanted to help."

Silence stretched.

"We're not getting back together."

"I hope not." Reggie sighed. "Look, after you broke it off, I thought you were finally figuring it out. You need to focus on you, not give in just because he promised you something. What did he promise?"

"No promises. He just mentioned wanting to get married."

"What?"

Bexley held the phone out as Reggie shouted. "You done?"

"Married? Are you kidding me?"

Gripping her side, Bexley sat up. "It's not happening, okay?"

"You don't sound all that convincing."

"I've had a bad few days," Bexley muttered. "To be honest,

I've wanted to curl up in a ball and fall asleep, just let it pass me by. Hearing someone say they want to take care of me, it was nice. But no, Tennison and I are over. I can't go back there."

"Well, if you want my opinion, maybe you should be looking to Evan for that kind of comfort."

Bexley scoffed.

"You don't think so? You can't tell me you're not attracted to him. *Any* woman would be attracted to him."

"I didn't say that."

"But you're still hung up on Tennison?"

Stifling a comment, Bexley clenched her jaw. Reggie didn't understand, didn't get it. She had a huge family with brothers and sisters, and her parents were there to support her. Bexley had no one, no family to give her that kind of support. Tennison was now offering everything she'd desired her whole life.

"Things didn't end well with Tennison. But until that point, things were good. He was a good guy, kind and really supportive."

"You love him, huh?"

"Maybe. But what happened with us, I can't go back. I'm not looking for that kind of relationship with anyone. Not even Evan."

"I think you're leaving something out."

Bexley grimaced. "Let's just say I've had a rededication of what my life should be. That means no more relationships."

"Not even if Hot Evan wanted to?"

"Regg ..."

Reggie's laughter made Bexley smile.

The thing was, Evan had helped her so much the past few days. He'd been a lifeline right when she needed him. But that didn't mean it would be something more.

"Just call if you need anything. I'm serious about taking off, I can do that if you need me to. That offer doesn't stand for just anyone."

"Thanks so much, Regg. I'll try to keep you in the loop."

"That would make me feel much better. I've got to go, talk to you later."

"Yeah, bye," Bexley mumbled as the phone call ended.

EVAN SLID FROM THE SUV, staring up at the large office complex.

Litigation Press was the largest firm in this part of Dallas. After checking a few leads Buck had on Arlo and coming up empty, Evan decided to stop by to see if he could have a face-to-face with Bexley's former boss.

Striding up the steps to the doors, he wondered if he could find someone to talk to about Bexley and why she had been fired. If her immediate boss was that impressed, then Jeff was right. There was something missing.

"Evan?"

He turned. "Reggie White."

Crossed arms, she glared at him from across the room. "What're you doing here and not at your office protecting Bexley?"

Clenching his jaw, he closed the gap. "Her being at our office isn't common knowledge. I'd like to keep it that way," he muttered.

Reggie's eyes narrowed. "You here to check up on Tennison?"

"Why would I be here to check up on him?"

"I heard you two met yesterday." Reggie let out a smirk.

"I guess you've had a conversation with Bexley recently. What else do you know?"

Reggie looked around and motioned to the doors. He followed her from the lobby, her straight black hair pulled back in a ponytail and swinging as she walked. She also had a large black backpack on.

"You on your way out?"

"I've got to get some things together for tomorrow, but it can wait."

Down the steps, she veered right and paused next to a couple of benches. Her eyes roaming, she finally spoke. "Tennison is Bexley's ex."

"I figured that," he mumbled.

"She wouldn't want me to tell you anything else about that. But the thing is, he's trying awfully hard to get back in her life, and that's a bad idea."

His jaw clenched tighter.

"Bexley lost her family, and she's been alone for a long time. I'm assuming you did your homework?"

He nodded.

"She's looking for a family, protection, security. I think that's what Tennison is offering, and no matter how badly it ended, I'm worried about her agreeing to whatever he's pushing." Her eyes went to the building briefly before looking to the parking lot. "She didn't deserve to be let go. I've been here five years, and she's the best we have when it comes to leadership. She does her job better than anyone else, without distraction. However, when it comes to her personal life, she's not as ... meticulous." Her big brown eyes met his. "I'm only telling you this so you'll understand."

"Understand what?"

She rolled her eyes. "Bexley can see bad news a mile away, a setup, an ambush long before it happens. But she can't read people close to her for anything. I read you just fine. If you want to act on all that, then be direct. Otherwise, she won't see it."

"Act on what? She's under our protection, and we'll do what we can to keep her safe. That's all."

Reggie nodded, taking a few steps until she was shoulder to shoulder with him. "Keep telling yourself that and you'll miss out. But I won't tell her if you're not going to." With a wink, she passed him by, heading back up the steps.

He tried unsuccessfully to relax his jaw. It struck him how

alone Bexley must feel if she were searching for all those things Reggie mentioned. But a friendship was about all he could offer her, nothing more. He needed to make space, separate himself from the situation. It wasn't that he could stop the attraction, but he could change the dynamic.

And that would have to happen soon.

22

Back at the office, Evan came in from the garage and found everyone once more at the kitchen island.

"We got an ID on the man he was talking to?" Evan asked the team as he settled into his seat.

"No, still trying to get a signal narrowed down. Arlo was on the move the entire time he was on the phone, and we're trying to single out the one number that matches each tower he was driving between." Sergio answered.

"Keep at it. Get the men who are unaccounted for from the warehouse and find them." Buck dropped a folder on the island. "Here's a list of known accomplices. We might try running them down and seeing if any are in the country."

"On it." Sergio headed back to the computers.

"What about Homeland? We need to see what's going on with the money trail." Evan glanced at Buck.

Buck handed him a few pages stapled together. "Here's what we've got, but it's not much. The accounts they've been watching seem to be draining, but nothing is being put back."

"So, he's definitely after something big." Jeff frowned.

"We need eyes on him. Keeping Bexley inside and safe will

only work for so long. We need to become proactive." Haiden started pacing.

"What's on your mind, Haiden?' Jeff looked him over with wide eyes, just as surprised as Evan that Haiden had strung together so many words at once.

"He has the money to do something big ... leaving the C-4 behind, maybe more than just an explosion. Sitting around and waiting won't do us any good."

"I agree. But we can't just go looking for him." Evan shrugged.

"Why not? We know what it takes to scout. We can start with some big-name targets and move down from there."

"Go for it. Start a list, and then tomorrow we'll all go and take a look."

Haiden nodded at Jeff.

"Let's remember to keep the pertinent information to ourselves, okay?" Buck pinned everyone with a look.

"I'm going to see if Bexley's hungry." Danica ascended the stairs, and Evan felt all eyes on him as he looked through the file folder in front of him.

"What?"

"Nothing, man." Jeff moved from the kitchen, and Evan noticed Haiden leaning against the counter.

"What do you want?"

Haiden just shrugged as his eyes drifted toward the stairs. Turning, Evan saw Danica helping Bexley make her way down.

He gathered up the paperwork and cleared a spot on the island, standing and pulling out the barstool before taking the stack of papers upstairs to the computer area.

"LET'S ORDER OUT." Jeff tossed a Thai menu on the island.

Danica lifted the menu as Bexley took the seat next to her.

Fighter

"I think a round of cards is called for after we eat," Danica mumbled as she studied the menu.

"Dominos." Haiden rested his elbows on the island, watching Danica.

"Fine, we can play dominoes." Danica rolled her eyes and took a long drink of her coke.

"I'm sure you guys are tired, we don't have to play anything." Bexley smiled as Jeff also leaned against the counter.

"No way, I'm up for a game, and this time, Haiden, you're going down."

Haiden huffed. "Keep dreaming, Jeff."

"You see what I have to deal with?" Danica motioned to the two men.

"Whatever. You're more competitive than all of us put together." Jeff grinned as he shoved his hands in his pockets.

"I am not." Danica's jaw dropped.

"Dani, seriously?" Haiden spoke up and Danica turned to glare at him.

Bexley muffled her laughter as Buck set down his phone and smiled. "Now, Danica, you can't even sit there and deny how competitive you are." Buck's gravelly voice was lighthearted.

She hadn't considered Buck and his place here. Obviously their leader, usually in the background, she assumed he kept the wheels moving. Jeff and Danica seemed to take the lead when there was conversation. But Buck, where did he fit in? How did they all know him?

"Fine, but just so you two know, you're way worse than me. Bex will see it first-hand."

"Oh no, don't put me in the middle." She chuckled as Danica bumped her arm.

"Come on, we've got to stick together. Otherwise, they'll gang up on us."

Bexley laughed out loud. "Agreed."

After eating, the rules were explained as Bexley, Danica, Jeff, and Haiden gathered around the large ottoman.

"So, if I do this ..." Bexley put her dominoes out in a row amid the groans of the others. "I win?"

"I don't believe you've never played Mexican Train dominoes before," Haiden mumbled.

She chuckled and added up everyone's scores. She had won all four rounds so far.

"I'm out. I need to go work out after driving around all day." Jeff stood.

"What about Buck or Evan? Would they want to play?" Bexley knew Sergio went home to see his wife and daughter for the evening.

Danica shook her head. "Nah, Buck doesn't play dominoes, and Evan is anti-social."

As he left, Jeff muffled a laugh at Danica's comment.

"What does that mean?" She looked to Danica.

"He's just solitary. He hasn't come out of his shell like me." Haiden flashed a quick grin. He had a great smile. Too bad he never used it.

"Out of your shell?" Danica chuckled. "No, that's not it. Look, Evan is a great teammate. But he's not interested in being 'friends.'" Danica motioned with her fingers. "It took us all of a month before we stopped trying."

"*You* stopped trying," Haiden interjected.

"I'm not going to get up and go invite him to play. If you want to, be my guest. But you know he'll just slam the door in your face."

Bexley frowned at Danica. "Why?"

"He's just that way." Danica shrugged as she racked up the dominoes to put in the tin.

Bexley leaned back against the couch.

Although she saw that anti-social behavior when they were all together, Evan had proven himself a different person with her. He'd been there when she broke down, helped with her pain, and given her comfort when she needed it. That Evan—he was a hero.

Fighter

It further proved her point that he had simply reacted with her. They were put in close contact, in a hostage situation where they had to depend on each other to come out safely. Even if he didn't want to admit it, he probably felt responsible for her.

Her phone buzzed, and Tennison's name flashed on the screen.

"Got a call?" Danica's eyebrow arched.

She hit end and slid it back into her pocket. "No one important," she mumbled.

God, help me to shake these feelings for Tennison. Reggie was right, and she doesn't even know just how bad it got. Open my eyes to see his true character, not react to the fact I'm alone.

"What now? Cards?"

She nodded as Danica stood, putting up the dominoes and returning with a deck of playing cards.

23

Bexley breathed out as the uncomfortable silence lingered in the vehicle. This was the sixth building site she and Evan watched the guys walk into then leave, shaking their heads.

"How long do we have to keep following Haiden and Jeff around?"

"Until Buck says we're done." Evan's tone was tight as he glared at her for a moment.

"Okay, so what're they doing?"

"Working."

She clenched her jaw. "Working on what?"

"Not my place to discuss it. It's not my call." He shook his head as his gaze went back to the window.

She groaned and tried to find a more comfortable position. After being in the car most of the day, chasing after the rest of the team, she regretted letting Danica talk her into coming along. She should've just stayed at the office, especially once Buck told her to get in the car with Evan.

Glancing at her phone, she noticed the missed calls and two voice messages. Not willing to pull them up where Evan might hear, she switched to her text messages.

I'm worried about you, Bex. Give me a call so we can talk. Love you.

She frowned and shut her phone off. Why couldn't she just ignore that pull? Was she that far gone when it came to Tennison?

Evan reached out to grab a water at her feet and she shrank away, pulling her arm up to protect her side. Evan froze, then she felt his fingers tapping her knee.

"Bex, come on. Time to talk." His easy tone made her blush as she realized just how badly she had reacted.

"I'm just frustrated and worked up, it makes everything worse," she muttered as she turned to look out the window, working to ignore the pull on her heart.

"That's not all of it. We can talk about anything. What about your work?"

She turned to see a simple smile on his face as he leaned over the console, his fingers still tapping her knee. She looked away again, shaking her head. Her past, all of it, wasn't a topic she wanted to discuss.

"I don't want to talk, Evan."

"You don't trust me?"

"I trust you to do your job. I know you're very good at your job." Her eyes met his.

"What about why you don't work in protective services anymore?"

Heat flushed her cheeks. "I'm not in the mood to talk about it."

His heavy sigh echoed.

"How about we discuss your aversion to hanging out with your co-workers?"

"We're not going there."

"You know, you can only be stand-offish for so long before no one wants to try anymore. Last night, we were playing dominoes, and I asked if you were going to join us. They laughed. No one

Fighter

even invited you because you never want to play. Apparently, you don't want to be friends." She shook her head at his glare. "Evan, you've already shown me how much more you can be. Why can't you let them see just a little of that?"

"I think we're done talking." His clenched response angered her.

"I'm trying here. Nothing makes you happy, does it?"

"Not really."

"And why is that?"

"Nothing I want to discuss."

"Really?"

He pinned her with narrowed eyes. "Yeah. That's an answer you should understand."

"Have a good afternoon?"

Bex glanced at Evan before she brushed past Jeff and headed upstairs, clutching her side and grunting with each step. Her door slammed shut as Evan went to the fridge and pulled out a Coke.

"So ... that was awkward. What happened?"

Evan glared at Jeff as he opened the drink and sipped it a minute before leaning against the counter.

"What happened last night?"

Jeff shrugged. "I don't know. I was in the weight room."

He frowned. Seemed Jeff wasn't the talker. Danica—she had no problems talking.

"What do you think happened last night?" Jeff leaned against the island, crossing his arms.

"Apparently, someone mentioned me while everyone was out here playing dominoes."

"Oh, you mean the fact you don't want anything to do with any of us?"

He glared at Jeff.

"What? That's who you are. That's the man you've reminded us you are over and over again." Jeff shrugged. "You've been here almost six months. You don't take time off to go and do anything, you live here full time and refuse to be a part of our team." Jeff paused and tapped his finger on the island. "You know, when Buck asked me about you joining our group, he gave me a file on you."

"What?" His hands fisted as he took a step toward Jeff.

"Look, 'most everything was redacted. I don't know even half of what happened your last mission out. But Buck wanted you here, and he wanted me to back up the decision. I read your eval and your action report. I still have it if you want to read it."

His heart pounded at the thought. "No, I don't. And I don't want anyone else to read it either."

That report, that last mission, it's what killed him.

"No one else will read it, Ev. But I agreed with Buck you would be a good fit, both for you and for us. But after six months and all the tests we've had as a group, I expected you to at least attempt to be part of our team."

"I am part of the team." He gritted his teeth, muttering the words as he tried to ease his temper.

"It's more than just showing up to work, you know that." Jeff shook his head. "Look, no one knows my past, I don't advertise it, and I don't expect you to either. I'm just saying take an interest when we're all together, find a way to connect. You and Haiden seem to have bonded, but that needs to be with all of us. No one is going to ask you anything, you know that, right?"

His jaw dropped as he worked to formulate some kind of answer, his anger finding its way to the surface.

"Don't blow up, Ev. Just trying to let you know that we see how hard you've worked to keep your distance." Jeff nodded and walked away as Evan stood dumbfounded.

24

Bexley tossed her phone on the desk and kicked off her shoes. Evan was the most frustrating man she'd been around in a long time. Picking her phone back up, she scrolled to her voicemail and listened.

"Bex, call me. I want to know where you are so I can come check on you. I love you, and I know you still love me. Call me back."

Frowning, she deleted the message. Tennison had never been so ... persistent. He wasn't that type. He liked it when women came to him, chased after him.

Why was he suddenly trying so hard? They'd broken up almost two months ago.

The phone vibrated, and an unknown name popped up.

"Hello?"

"Bexley."

His hissed voice rang out as she rushed out of the room and paused at the top of the steps. "What do you want?"

She motioned to Evan and Jeff, pointing at her phone.

"Your help."

Evan pulled out his own phone, his fingers flying over the keys.

"I told you, you missed that opportunity when you left me at the warehouse to die."

Sergio and Danica came running from behind her, handing an assault rifle to Evan as they ran down the steps. Evan grabbed her waist and aided her down the steps, then disappeared.

"It was my mistake, really. I should've had the foresight to keep you around longer. We could accomplish great things, Bexley."

"I would never do anything with you or for you." Her body trembled as Jeff stood in front of her, motioning to keep talking.

"Tell me, why're you even here? Why did you attack the mall, and what did you need so badly that you would kill for it? It's just a mall."

His chuckle sounded as she hobbled to the kitchen, pushing speaker on the phone, and setting it on the island. Jeff had his laptop opened, her phone number entered into a box as the screen pinged the location.

"I have my reasons. Many, actually. One thing you should know about me is that I'm highly intelligent. I stay several steps ahead of the competition, so to speak. Who's there with you? Friends?"

Jeff gave a thumbs up, mouthing, "we have a location."

"What friends? And for the record, I wouldn't say intelligent."

"Why, Bexley, do you doubt me?"

She was about to retort when the call ended. Her gaze jumped to Jeff. "It's a trap, isn't it?"

Jeff tapped the Bluetooth earpiece. "Buck, he's got something planned. Be on alert." Jeff nodded. "They know, Bexley. They're prepared for this. I'll be on with Buck the whole time."

She leaned into the island, exhausted. After the argument with Evan and rushing up and down the steps, her body was spent and her head ached.

"If he's still at the location, we'll get him. Don't worry."

"I know, but still. This guy is ... I'm not sure why he's doing all this. A distraction?"

Jeff shrugged. "Could be. But we're secure here, and the team knows what to look for. I heard Buck call in the police, so they'll have help."

Laying her forehead on an arm, she closed her eyes.

God, please keep them all safe.

"So, you've led them straight to us?"

Arlo ignored the young man at his side.

"I'm leaving."

"No, you're staying." Arlo cut his eyes at the younger mercenary. "As they head back to their office, I need you to follow. Report in where they reside."

"We can just grab one of them if you want that information. We don't need all this where we can easily be caught."

Arlo stood. "You either follow my plans, or you don't get paid. Those are your options."

The young man huffed, rushing down the fire escape from the roof of the apartment building.

Looking over the roads, Arlo smiled as several SUVs appeared a few blocks out. He checked his watch and made notes of the time and direction. He zoomed his binoculars in on the men, immediately identifying the man who had taken Bexley.

"What now? Let them catch us?" The bearded man beside him grumbled.

"The explosives we've planted should give them enough distraction." Arlo held the cell phone out, waiting. "We now know which direction the team came from and how long it took them to arrive. I have all I need should your associate fail to tail the SUVs back to the holding location. That is, if anyone survives."

"He's new," the bearded man huffed. "I doubt he can keep up."

"Then we won't need him." Arlo straightened, glaring at the bearded man. "I've got more men coming in the morning anyway."

As police cars arrived, he waited until it appeared as if most of the officers had entered the building. He hit a button on the phone.

The explosion blew the top of the building, shattering windows as debris filled the air.

25

Evan tucked himself into a ball as the building wavered.

"Evan?" Buck's voice echoed from the hallway.

"I'm good. Get out before the building collapses!"

Evan stood, bracing himself against the wall and staggering outside. Buck gripped his arm and pulled him aside. Taking a deep breath, the fresh air filled Evan's lungs. The debris finally cleared as officers filled the back alleyway.

"Anyone else get caught?" Evan looked up at Buck.

"No. You seeing that barrel that matched the ones in the warehouse saved us."

Evan shook his head. "Any word on Arlo?"

"Not yet. They've got cell phone jammers installed, so I've not received any reports yet. If he's here, we'll find him."

Evan straightened and followed the crowd from the alley. Searching the buildings overhead, Arlo could've been in any of the taller structures, seen them coming, and been clear of the blast.

Were they targets now too?

"Well?"

Bexley stood as Danica entered, tossing a dirt-covered cap on her desk.

"Everyone's good. The blast took off the top of the building but didn't cripple it. There wasn't enough C-4 to take it down. A few bumps and bruises, but we're all okay."

"Thank goodness," Bexley muttered as she collapsed on her bed.

"Jeff's with Buck, going over the report, but there's no sign of Arlo or anyone suspicious. Evan and Haiden are helping to search the area, just to make sure there aren't any more devices."

"And how do they know if there are?" Bexley questioned.

Danica shrugged. "Something about the barrels used in the warehouse? Evan noticed one pushed up against the wall on the first floor once we entered. It wasn't until we hit the second floor that he could smell it and ordered an evac."

"The motor oil. I smelled that in the warehouse. I just assumed it was the building, not the explosives," Bexley mumbled.

She leaned back against the wall. Perched on her bed, she closed her eyes and exhaled. Between hearing Jeff's description of the entry and Evan telling everyone to get out, she was emotionally spent.

"You okay?"

"Not really. Hearing what happened, Jeff yelling for a report, it was like time stood still." Holding her head, she sighed. "I've got a massive headache now."

Danica pulled up a chair next to Bexley's bed. "Hey, we're all good. You want me to get something for you?"

"No, it's fine," Bexley mumbled. "And to think I was so irritated with Evan and now, after this, it seems so pointless."

"What happened?"

"I asked what the plan was, what we were doing today. He wouldn't tell me, and it was just frustrating."

"I'm not sure what his deal is. We're just looking for the next attack, seeing if we can figure it out before Arlo sets up. But after today, I'm not sure we're going to get ahead of him."

Bexley nodded.

"Evan did mention something last night I thought was odd."

"What's that?"

Danica grinned. "Something about your boyfriend?"

Bexley's jaw dropped. "What? What boyfriend?"

"He just mentioned he thought you had one. He didn't seem all that excited about it."

Surely, he didn't think she and Tennison were still together. Not after the way she reacted on the porch yesterday and Evan told him to leave.

"No boyfriend, and I don't think someone like Evan would care anyway."

"I don't know, macho attitudes like his ..."

Bexley huffed. "I guess that's an accurate description for all these guys."

"Well, when it comes to Haiden, I'm not so sure macho is the term I would use for him." Danica leaned back in her desk chair, a smirk on her face as she tapped her lip with the eraser of the pencil.

"Oh? What term would you use?"

"Brooding, maybe." Danica winked, and Bexley laughed out loud. "But with Evan, he's all business all the time. I've tried to joke with him, but he doesn't go along. Apparently, it's not just me."

"Maybe you should ask Haiden what his deal is?" Bexley winked.

Danica flushed. "Not worth the energy. Evan does his job, and that's all I need. If he doesn't want to be friends, I guess I can live with that."

Bexley leaned to her side with a grunt. "So, tell me about the ATF. Why did you quit?"

"I enjoyed the job itself. But I refused to do undercover OPS, making things ... complicated."

"Sorry. You don't have to talk to about it."

"I'm good. I've had my head on straight for a while. I am worried about you, though." Danica hesitated. "What you've had to deal with, you need someone to talk to. And by someone, I mean a professional, not Evan or me."

"Me? I'm fine. I've been down the therapy road, I just needed to get back to God's road. Besides, I don't think I'll be talking to Evan for a while." Bexley pulled at the cuff of her long-sleeved shirt. "I'm with you. I can expect him to do his job, he's good at that."

"You don't want something more?"

Bexley shook her head. "That was one of the things that pulled me the wrong direction."

Danica nodded. "Happens to the best of us. But that doesn't mean something with him couldn't be different. I mean if he felt the same way."

Bexley shrugged. "Not the right time. I've got my own baggage to deal with."

"That's why I mentioned a therapist. I think you deserve some help."

"Maybe." Bexley glanced up. "What about with you, ever experience workplace romance?"

Danica scoffed. "Yeah."

"Why do you think I'm now a part-time librarian?"

Danica's jaw dropped. "What? Is that what happened?"

Bexley shrugged. "Yeah, he wasn't my boss. But high enough up it didn't take long for a pink slip to find its way to me."

"Was it worth it?"

"It had its moments ..." Bexley trailed off, her jaw clenching. "But in the end, I lost my career, which was the one thing that held me together for so long."

"I would say mine wasn't either, but he's a good guy. It just came to a decision, and the decision wasn't mine to make."

"So not even if Haiden ..."

Danica groaned. "Workplace romance never works. Besides,

he's a good friend, one I wouldn't want to lose if things go south."

"Why do you assume they'll go south?"

"They always do, don't they?"

Bexley chuckled. "I guess."

"You know what we need now?"

"What's that?"

"Cookie dough." Danica grinned.

Bexley laughed as they headed out the door and down the hallway, pausing at the top of the stairs. Surrounding the ottoman, all the men had gathered with laptops and file folders. All eyes watched them as they paused. Hers, of course, found Evan's before she could stop herself.

"See, what did I tell you?" Danica whispered in her ear.

"What's that supposed to mean?" Jeff stood as they headed down the stairs, Danica taking her time and not leaving Bexley behind.

Danica shrugged. "Nothing, just a little girl talk."

"Come on with that. Girl talk," Sergio scoffed.

"What, like you guys don't talk when we're not around?" Danica countered.

Bexley barely heard the sounds of 'no' and 'of course not' coming from the group of men. As she took the stairs, something shifted in her side, and the pain worked its way through her body. With every step, she felt her body falling, dizziness flooding her vision.

Making it to the kitchen, she slid onto the stool, leaning against the island and holding her aching head.

"What's wrong?" Evan muttered.

She glanced up and, finding him without any injury, the guilt of being irritated with him earlier disappeared. "I'm sore."

"You were fine earlier, what did you do?"

She glared. "I didn't *do* anything."

"Then why is it worse now than it was when we got home?"

"Look, I ..." she paused to see the entire group watching their little show. She cleared her throat. "I'm fine."

"So, what are you guys talking about? Does it not include us?" Danica's sarcastic tone echoed, shifting the focus once more.

Bexley's vision cleared and the dizziness and pain ebbed.

"We were just going over an update from Homeland. There's been some chatter, and Arlo's name was mentioned."

Danica perched on the arm of the couch, but Bexley found herself watching Haiden for his reaction. After seeing Danica's face flush every time she mentioned him, she wondered if it went both ways.

Haiden had his focus on Buck, but he had already stolen a few glances at Danica.

Maybe it did.

"No target, just Arlo's name. So we might be doing another sweep tomorrow."

She didn't hear the rest of Buck's words as she laid her head down on the island. Another day in the car *not* talking to Evan, perfect. Now she really did need that cookie dough.

She glanced up at Evan's back leaning against the island only a few feet from her, his focus on Buck and the team. Sure he was protective of her, but there was no way he was as thrown by her as Danica and Reggie thought.

"Bexley? Did you hear me?"

She focused on the group as she tried to straighten at the sound of Buck's voice. "I'm sorry, what?"

"We might need you to stay here and work on a few things." Buck was watching intently.

"Sure, just tell me what I can do to help." She looked up to Danica, who had her eyes focused past her shoulder.

As much as Bexley wanted to turn to see what Danica was looking at, she didn't have to. The back of her neck tingled, and she knew Evan was watching.

Buck had a few more things to say, but she barely listened. Her body hurt, and she wanted to lie down.

"Finally." Danica came running past her and opened the fridge, pulling out a drawer. "You have got to be kidding me. Who cleaned out my drawer?"

Danica marched to the living room red-faced. "You." Danica pointed at Jeff.

"What?" Jeff looked like a deer caught in headlights.

If looks could kill, Jeff would be a goner.

"You're the one eating all the yogurt that is now in my drawer. You threw away my stuff?"

"What stuff? A half-eaten package of cookie dough is stuff?"

Danica tapped her foot on the floor. "Fine. I'm running to the store, anyone want anything?"

"I'll go with you." Bexley was trying to stand when Evan's hand gripped hers.

Snatching her hand away, she glared.

"You have to stay here," he mumbled.

Her jaw clenched as she fought her anger. "I don't want her to go alone."

"I'm a big girl too." Danica winked.

"I'll go. I've got to pick up some stuff." Haiden's deep voice sounded.

Bexley could barely contain her smile as she sat back down, ignoring Evan. Danica tossed her a knowing glance as she and Haiden headed out the door.

"I saw that." Jeff stood in front of her with a grin.

She shrugged. "Saw what?"

"I know what you did there." He sauntered up with his hands shoved into his pockets.

"What's he talking about?"

She turned to frown at Evan's smirk. "I have no idea."

Ignoring his glare, she worked herself to standing before trying to take a few steps toward the stairs. Why couldn't she shake this dizzy feeling? She just needed some more rest. Maybe she could get upstairs unnoticed and lie down for a bit.

"Miss Bowers, a word." Buck headed toward her. So much for going back to bed.

"I told you, Bex or Bexley."

"My mistake." He led her down the hallway for some privacy. "Bexley, you do know we're here to help you, right?"

"Of course, I wouldn't be here if I didn't think that." She leaned against the wall, nausea working its way through her body at the pain pulsing through her head and side.

"Look, it's none of my business what's going on with you and Evan, but if it interferes with us getting our work done, it becomes my business."

"Sir, what are you talking about?" At first, she thought it was the pain making her misunderstand him, but he was serious about something.

"What's wrong?" Buck tilted his head to the side.

"I don't know, I ..." she took a breath. "I'm just a little dizzy..."

She leaned her head against the wall, vision blurring. Then her body went weightless as consciousness dimmed.

26

"What happened?" Danica's voice quaked as it echoed down the hallway.

Evan turned to see Danica running toward him, Haiden at her heels.

"She passed out after you left. Doctor says her rib is fractured and that concussion is hanging on. He thinks it's causing her to black out."

"Is she going to be okay?"

Evan had never seen Danica so worked up before, her face flushed and her eyes wide.

"Yeah, she just needs to rest, and she needs to ask for help."

"I really don't think it was bothering her that much. And she has been resting. What do you think she's doing up there?"

He shook his head with a huff.

"I'll stay here tonight."

His jaw clenched. She held his gaze, arms crossed and determined.

"You're too irritated to stay here."

"Irritated? Why would I be irritated?"

"She mentioned that little spat in the car earlier. You know, where you wouldn't tell her what we were doing all day today?"

"It was nothing."

Danica started to argue when Haiden cut in.

"Danica, he's good. Let's get back."

She looked past Evan, pausing a moment, and then nodded, throwing a quick warning glare before pushing past. Evan looked to Haiden, who gave him the same glare.

"I guess you have some explaining to do."

Evan shook his head at Buck and kept pacing as they waited for the doctor to come out.

"Wha ..." Bexley struggled to speak, but her throat burned. She gave up, closing her eyes as dizziness took over.

"Hey, get the nurse." Evan's voice came through and she realized she was in a hospital bed. Again.

"What happened?" She furrowed her eyebrows and felt him grip her fingers, holding them gently as his thumb moved over her knuckles.

"You passed out."

"Why?" She worked to open her eyes, but the light was killing her. Raising her left hand pulled like a lead weight as she tried to shield her eyes.

"Hang on."

He moved her arm back down, and the light over her head went off.

"Thanks." Her voice wavered as she worked to control more emotions bubbling to the surface.

Lord, give me some strength to hold it in!

"Now, why did I pass out?" She finally opened her eyes to see Evan sitting next to her, looking concerned and awfully heroic once again.

"The doctor thinks your rib is fractured, and you've still got a concussion." His jaw clenched and she closed her eyes, not wanting to see his frustration.

"Now, I'm so glad you're awake." A sickly sweet tone flowed through the air, and a nurse with long blond hair appeared at her bedside. "Let's check your vitals, okay? Her arm was pulled up as the cuff was slid to her bicep."

"Blood pressure and heart rate a little high, but that's to be expected. Oxygen looks great. Now, let's remove this and see how you feel."

The nurse removed a tube pushing oxygen into her nose. Tugging from Evan's hand, she found the button on the frame and raised her head a little.

"Just let me know if you need anything."

Bexley nodded and saw the nurse watching Evan for approval as well.

"Sir, can I get you anything?"

"I'm good." He didn't even look her way, and she huffed as she left.

Bexley smirked before she could stop it.

"That's obviously not for me. Why are you suddenly smiling?" His terse tone made her sigh as she raised her head some more, finding it easier to wake.

"Nothing." She wiped her face and pushed back her hair, pleased to see she was still in her own clothes and not a gown. "So, when do I leave?"

"The doctor ordered some other tests, we might be here a while." He stood and started pacing.

"I'll be fine. You can go."

He paused and shook his head, then resumed his course. Sighing, she found herself ready to unload when he suddenly turned and gripped the bedframe at her feet.

"You really don't want me here?" Even with his hat down low, she could easily see his frustration.

"You're the one who gets bothered by having to partner with me all the time. Today, in the car? Silent, then irritated. I can tell you're annoyed. " She bit her tongue and waited.

His jaw moved back and forth as his hands finally released

the frame. He sat down next to her, then stood and moved closer, pulling her right hand into his.

"That's not it."

"Then what's your problem? Why did you get so bothered by me today?"

"Look, you tend to make an argument out of everything." He sighed. "Earlier, you said I should try and be more like who I've been around you." His words forced. "So, what about you? I know there's a different side to you too."

She sat herself up in the bed with a groan. "I'm not sure what's going on, but you're so different when it's just us and then today, getting all irritated." She licked her lips, trying to find the words. "All I know is that I've got my own baggage to deal with, and everyone keeps saying …"

"Saying what?"

She leaned back, crossing her arms. That was a discussion she didn't want to get into.

He watched her for a moment. "Okay, we don't have to get into that if you don't want to. But what baggage are you talking about? Your family?"

She nodded. "I've always looked for ways to fill that void, and I'm just the most terrible judge of character," she muttered.

"You're not so bad." A smirk sat on his handsome face.

"Thanks," she chuckled.

"You do argue with me all the time. Why?"

She shrugged. "I don't know. I guess I'm used to being in charge, understanding what's going on."

He tapped at her knee and she uncrossed her arms, laying her hand over his. Staring down at him gently holding her fingers once more pulled at her.

"Why do you always do that?" she whispered.

"What?"

"You always reach out when it's just us, give me that little bit of something …" She trailed off, not knowing how to finish that sentence without it revealing a little too much.

He cleared his throat. "Look, I can be friends, but that's it. I'm not ... I've got so much stuff, and I—"

"You're telling me you have baggage?" She narrowed his eyes as he sighed. "Just for the record, I'm not looking either. I can't do that right now."

"Oh?" He tilted his head. "I thought there was something more going on with that guy."

"No." She pulled her hand free. "He's not ... I mean, he's one of the reasons I'm not looking right now. Because we just broke up."

"That's all?" His cobalt eyes stared. "Because I think there's much more to that story."

Shifting in the bed, she clasped her hands together in her lap. "Not looking to talk about that," she whispered. "When I was sitting with that bomb, all I could think of was all my mistakes, and he was one of them. I'm not looking to keep making that same mistake."

"I can understand that. Not wanting to make the same mistake." He stood and paced.

Waiting him out, he finally turned, his lips a narrow line. "Mine wasn't a bomb, but it was enough to remind me what not to do."

"What happened?"

He glanced at the door and then leaned into the foot of her bed.

"Three years ago, I got involved with a woman who didn't have the best intentions." He narrowed his gaze. "I was deployed overseas, so when I kept getting emails and letters from her I ignored them. Once I got home, there was an oversized envelope containing a paternity test."

Bexley's eyes went wide as she waited, a lump forming in her throat.

"It turned out to be negative, but the situation rocked my world. Made me realize I couldn't continue living that life. I got back into Bible studies with some of the guys on base." He shook his head. "Working helps me stay focused. The job, it's who I am, and I need that connection. Bexley, I want to be friends, but that's it. I can't do more."

"Agreed." She leaned back, pushing on her side.

"What's wrong?"

"I guess it's pulling again, I feel a spasm or something," she muttered.

Lifting her left arm, she brought it over her chest in front of her, trying to stretch out. Evan made his way to her left side, eyebrows furrowed.

The spasm got worse as she turned to her right, blowing out at the pain from her rib and her sore muscles.

"Stop moving around. Here, lean back." He gently tugged on her shoulder until she leaned back into the bed. He reached around to her back and worked the angry muscle, rubbing it into submission as she tried to relax in the bed. "Better?"

"Yeah, thanks," she whispered.

Closing her eyes, her body relaxed. Just feeling him near seemed to calm her instantly, his cologne wafting around her and making her stifle a grin.

Coming back to reality, she straightened as Evan's hand slowed and moved from behind her back.

Evan leaned back and cleared his throat. "You want some pain medicine?"

"Not yet, I'll take something before I lie down tonight." She opened her eyes to see him watching. "What?"

"I really thought you and that Tennison guy were a couple."

Her face heated. "No. We were together for almost six months. But I broke it off."

"You want to talk about it?"

She shook her head, closing her eyes. Relaxing into the bed, she could feel him watching, but for the first time since they met, it was a comforting thought.

27

As the doctor came in with Buck, Evan moved to the wall, waiting to hear the plan.

"You should be fine, but your movements need to be limited. Fill that prescription, and you can use ice to help with the pain. Keep your heart rate down and no unnecessary movements. That concussion will ground you quicker than you think."

Bexley nodded. "So I can leave?"

"As long as you're going to take it easy. If you end up back here again, we might have to keep you longer than a few hours."

She nodded with a grin. She had a great smile. He leaned his head back against the wall and exhaled. After finally getting everything out in the open, there was no reason to feel the same kind of pull. She wasn't with Tennison, but she wasn't looking for anything more. So why did he still feel so intrigued with her?

"Okay, honey, there you go. Take care and remember to keep from moving around too much."

The blond-headed nurse put a Band-Aid on Bexley's arm where she had taken out the IV. Bexley nodded and found him watching, a smirk suddenly appearing on her face. He narrowed his eyes.

What is that for?

"Hope you guys have a nice rest of the night."

The blond nurse suddenly had a hold of his arm, grinning up at him.

Oh, great.

He forced a smile and nod as heat rocked his face. His attention went back to Bexley. She was covering her mouth and clearly holding in her laughter. She started to chuckle when the nurse finally left, then winced.

"What was so funny?"

A chuckle sounded from his left. His head snapped around to see a grin on Buck's face.

"Are you that oblivious? That little nurse has been trying to get your attention all evening."

Another giggle erupted, and he looked back to Bexley holding her side.

"I'm glad everyone finds that so amusing." He allowed a grin to slip out as he stepped toward Bexley, who was attempting to get out of bed by herself. "Easy, you should wait for the wheelchair."

"I'll be fine."

He held her elbow, keeping her steady.

"I'll get the car pulled around."

Evan nodded to Buck. The door opened and a gasp had him turning to see Tennison, minus the suit.

"Tennison?"

"Bex? Are you okay?" He rushed inside and Evan held his ground, doing his best to keep from escorting the guy from the room.

Bexley's face went crimson. "What're you doing here? How did you know?"

Tennison reached out and Bexley stepped back. "Someone saw you and called. What happened? Did that guy get to you? I told you we needed to set up professional help."

That's it.

"Take a hike—"

"Evan."

He glanced down at Bexley.

"Can you give us a second?"

"I don't think that's a good idea," Evan mumbled.

The look on her face, Tennison's intrusion into her space ... Reggie's words echoed in Evan's mind.

"If she wants to talk—"

"Tennison." Bexley's clipped voice cut the man off. She motioned to Evan and he released her elbow, walking to the other side of the room where he would be available should she need him.

"Seriously? He's not going to leave?" Tennison glared, but Evan just stared back.

"I don't think you should be here." Bexley's low voice barely sounded in the room.

Tennison turned back to her. "I told you I love you, that I want to marry you. I'm not leaving you like this."

Wait, what? Marriage? Reggie was right. Tennison was pushing for something.

"You told me all this two months *after* I broke up with you and after ... everything else," she murmured.

Tennison's neck turned red. "You didn't give me a chance to discuss it. You just left."

Bexley's jaw clenched as she gripped her elbows.

"I deserve another chance. You know I do. We can't just throw all this away simply because I made a mistake."

"Mistake?" Bexley's voice broke.

The way she pulled away, shrank back whenever people got too close, did Tennison do that to her?

Tennison stepped in, taking hold of Bexley's hand. Clenching his jaw, Evan forced himself to stay in place.

"I want to take care of you. That's what you said you always wanted, family. I can be that for you."

Tears rolled down her face. "I have to go."

Evan took that as his queue.

"Bexley, I'm not just letting you walk away." Tennison had her cornered.

Pushing between them, he faced Tennison.

"She and I are together. You're interfering," Tennison growled.

"I'm not the one making her cry," Evan mumbled, barely able to contain the need to physically counter Tennison's remark. "She's leaving, and you're going to let her go. No more calls or visits."

"Or what?" Tennison sneered. "I've got more money and lawyers at my call than I know what to do with. I can mess with you just for fun. Besides, it's not like someone like *you* can give her what she wants."

Evan felt a pull on the back of his shirt. "We're leaving."

Bexley slid from behind him, and he stepped with her, keeping between her and Tennison as they reached the door.

She turned. "Goodbye, Tennison. I don't ... Please don't call anymore."

As they stepped from the room, an aide stood outside with a wheelchair.

"I've got it," Evan mumbled as he helped Bexley into the seat.

Bexley softly sobbed in the chair as he wheeled her into the elevator. Squeezing her shoulder, he exhaled angrily at Tennison trying to guilt her into a relationship. She'd just admitted wanting a family, someone to take care of her, then Tennison comes in and says he's ready to give it to her?

What a jerk.

His face heated. "Bex? Did he—"

"I don't want to talk about," she mumbled between sobs.

If he ever saw that guy again ...

"You told him you're not with Tennison?" Danica's brown eyes danced.

"Yeah, didn't really have a choice since Tennison showed up at the hospital."

"What?" Danica's jaw dropped.

"I have no idea how he knew, but he showed up. Evan didn't want to leave, Tennison made a scene, and ..." Bexley couldn't believe Tennison was still pushing so hard for them to get back together.

"And?"

Bexley glanced up at Danica. "I left." She bit her lip, leaning back in the chair. Getting into details about Tennison's comments wasn't something she wanted to relive, and she knew Evan's life-altering moment was deeply personal as well. Just like hers.

"And what did Evan say?"

"About what?"

Danica huffed. "He was worried, wouldn't leave the hospital. Did you two discuss anything else?"

Bexley smirked. "Yes. But neither of us is looking for more. Just friends, and that's all I need."

"Okay." Danica shrugged. "I guess I'm surprised about Evan. Just the way he looks at you all the time."

Thank goodness Danica didn't ask for more details.

"Anyway, what about you? How did shopping go with Haiden?"

"I knew you did that on purpose." Danica tossed a pillow at her. "It was fine."

She chuckled. "You're blushing."

"Look, I've been down that same busted-up road you've been down. I want a relationship someday, but I'm not looking that close to home. Things always end up messy."

"I'm sorry for pushing it. But we can always dream, can't we?"

"It'll come along in God's timing." Danica paused and

watched her a moment. "I guess it's good that you two finally talked it out. But I'm not sure it's going to change much."

Bexley shrugged. "I have to admit, just because we talked it out doesn't make the attraction go away."

"No, I bet it didn't." Danica laughed as Bexley felt her face go hot.

28

"Seriously, man, it's not there." Evan was working hard to convince Sergio and Jeff there was nothing going on between him and Bexley.

"I saw you when she dropped. You were worried."

"So I can't be worried about her passing out?" He glared at Jeff.

Sergio chuckled. "You're the first person she goes to and the one she's comfortable with. You mentioned she doesn't like to be led, but you've had a hold of her I don't know how many times, and I've never seen her flinch."

"That's true." Jeff pointed to Sergio. "And I know first-hand how she doesn't like to be touched. But you, I've never seen her react when you help."

"Back off, guys."

Sergio, Jeff, and Evan stared at Haiden. The ever-quiet man rarely leaped into personal conflict, but Evan was grateful he chose now to speak up.

"You have something to add?" Jeff smirked.

"He's vexed. She is too. It can go both ways."

"And what does that mean?" Sergio shook his head.

Haiden took a deep breath. "God's got a plan for them. And

until then, they're going to have to find a way to deal with whatever's got them so worked up and wait it out until God says it's time."

"Whatever's got them worked up? I think we all know what that is." Sergio chuckled as did the others, even Haiden.

"And what about you and Danica?"

A muffled sound rolled through Jeff and Sergio, and Evan grinned. If they wouldn't drop it, he could shift the focus from himself to Haiden.

"Nothing. We're friends and colleagues. We have mutual respect." Haiden glared.

"That's it, Quiet Man?" Jeff grinned and Evan sat back to allow the man the floor. "What was it that had you running to the store, then?"

"I wanted to go to the store, and you think I felt the need to go with Danica?"

"Yes." Jeff just nodded and crossed his arms.

"You two do hang out a lot." Sergio grinned.

"I told you—friends. I hang out with you guys too."

Evan chuckled.

"What, Ev?" Haiden mumbled.

"I just remember hearing something the other day."

"When you were ... eavesdropping?" Haiden muttered.

Evan raised his eyebrows. "I told you, I was waiting to talk to Bexley. I just heard some things."

"I don't want to know." Haiden's jaw almost broke free from his face as tight as he was clenching it. He had a square jaw anyway, and Evan could easily see the tendons and muscles contracting.

"Man, you two got it bad!" Sergio started laughing and Jeff joined in.

"What about you, Jeff?" Haiden questioned.

"What about me? I'm the gentleman of the group, the lone wolf." Jeff's grin widened.

Fighter

"You say I spend a lot of time with Danica, but you two are together all the time." Haiden's gaze narrowed.

"Come to think of it, that's true." Evan sat back against the wall and put his gaze on Jeff, who nervously shifted.

"We're usually working out the cases and setting up details. Besides, I've known Danica for a long time."

"How long?" Haiden sounded more than a little interested.

"Look, she's more like a sister to me. That's how long." Jeff shrugged and headed to his room down the hallway.

"That was strange." Sergio looked between Evan and Haiden. "You know, come to think of it, I've never heard how Buck got Jeff or Danica on board. Just that he knew them."

Evan stood to head to the fridge and found a Coke. "You think there's more there?"

"Yeah, I think there is."

"Don't go digging, Serg. That's not our place." Haiden's forced tone appeared again.

"I don't dig on teammates, Haiden, you know that."

"I'm headed to bed." Evan tossed the can in the recycling bin and headed down the hallway to his room, his mind rolling with thoughts of Bex and what he could do to work through his emotions.

"Good grief," he muttered as he slammed the door, wishing the talk had fixed everything.

Hearing Tennison's comments about marriage and knowing how her previous relationship with him ended was building up something inside. He wanted to fix all the problems in her life, give in to all that attraction, and be *that* guy who could give her more.

"Anytime you want to step in, God. Anytime," he muttered.

29

"So what's the plan today?" Bex saddled up to the bar in the kitchen, the smell of breakfast in the air.

She spent a full day in bed yesterday, forgetting all about Tennison and how much he said he loved her and wanted to marry her. Mostly.

"We're going on a manhunt, and you're staying in bed." Danica bustled around the kitchen, pulling out biscuits from the oven and setting out bacon and eggs on the island.

Bexley groaned. "But I was in bed all day yesterday. I'm so bored. Surely there's something I can do."

"Sure. Rest. While you do that, we're going to run down a lead with the FBI."

Bexley puffed out a breath and laid her head on the island, only feeling a slight pull. She had to admit, being in bed all day had made her side feel better and her dizziness had ebbed. Sitting up, she turned slightly to see Evan come into the kitchen.

Dressed in his usual hat and cargo pants, he had on a black T-shirt that stretched across his broad chest. His perfectly trimmed beard outlined the beginnings of a grin forming on his lips. She turned back to the food and grabbed a piece of bacon to munch, forcing herself to find another focus.

He looked good. That attraction spiked, and suddenly all the comments everyone else had been making about Evan and the way he acted with her came to light.

"Bexley, how're you feeling today?" He paused at the island, and she smiled up at him.

"I'm fine."

"Fine, huh?" He turned around and leaned against the counter with his mug.

"Yes, I do feel better today. But I'm bored."

"She wants to go with us."

Bexley rolled her eyes at Danica's comment.

"No."

"I wasn't asking you. I asked Danica." Bexley narrowed her eyes.

"And I said no."

With a huff, Bexley stacked a plate with a biscuit and some eggs, then grabbed a water bottle from the fridge. Easing slowly up the stairs, she jumped as pressure pushed across her lower back.

"It's just me, easy," Evan muttered as he took the plate. "Why don't you hold the rail?"

She took his advice and finally made the landing. "Thanks, I'm good."

Evan kept walking and opened her door. She made her way inside and set down her water bottle as he handed her the plate.

"You taking it easy?"

"Yes, of course."

"I'm worried about you." He stood there, hands on his hips. "You don't sound like you're okay."

She shrugged. "I'm just in a bad mood. I'm not used to sitting around doing nothing. I feel less than useless, and I don't deal well with that." She grunted as she sat at the table, pulling her hair from her face.

"Look, I understand. I'll talk to Buck and see if he has anything you can work on, okay?"

Fighter

Her chin dropped as she fought to cover her surprise. "Really? You think he has something I can actually do?"

"I don't know." He smiled and shook his head. "I'll text you later." He turned to head out the door and paused, looking back, gripping the doorknob. "I'm glad you're feeling better today. Danica said you were in bed reading all day. I figured you didn't want company."

"I ... I was, but it would be nice to have some company every now and then." She smirked as he chuckled.

"I'll remember that next time." He turned and shut the door, leaving her once again surprised.

DRIVING TO THE AIRPORT, Evan ignored the need to focus on Bex. She had looked way too good this morning. Her rusty hair down and the way the leggings and tunic fit her body just right.

He sighed. The focus was on the airfield they were driving to, and that's what he needed to be thinking about, not Bex's amazing figure.

The FBI called Buck, stating a private jet listed a few red flag passengers. Aliases of the men from Arlo's heist. Although the TRT was only here for backup, Evan felt a weight lift off his shoulders.

Bexley needed to be safe, and they'd had no leads on Arlo's whereabouts or his plans until now. This bust could change everything.

"Who's going in with us?" He unbuckled his seatbelt and slid from the SUV.

"FBI said it's our lead if we want it. They get first shot at interrogations, though." Buck met him at the back, strapping on their protective gear and loading up with ammunition.

"That's fine by me. Never was any good at interrogations."

"I've noticed."

He grinned as Buck chuckled.

"Okay, you two, enough playing around. Some of us are in a tight space and would like to get this thing done and over with." Danica's voice came through their coms, and he snickered.

She and Haiden ended up on the roof of the adjoining building. Buck wanted Haiden covered so he could focus on their targets. Danica, however, was not that crazy about lying across a rooftop that was basically a tin building on the small airstrip.

"We'll be ready. We can't make them come any faster, Dani," Evan muttered as he finished with his gear.

The plan was for him and Buck to take the cockpit and Sergio and Jeff to cover the back. With trained mercenaries, they had to be careful and alert. That's why Haiden had them covered.

They were all set and waiting when Buck received a phone call.

"What?" Buck's whispered, annoyed.

Evan watched Buck's face fall.

"What's going on?" he whispered as Buck put up his phone.

"A bigger name popped, and the FBI believe he's on the way here."

"So, they want us to what? Step down?"

"Not exactly. We wait until FBI breeches first."

Evan grunted as Buck waved him off.

"Listen up everyone, we're to back off. FBI has a stake here, we're now in the passenger seat. Keep them covered."

Groans echoed in the coms.

He and Buck met up with Sergio and Jeff behind the hangar.

"We just need to keep eyes on everyone and be at the ready."

"Great." Evan shook his head, irritated that the operation was being handed over.

"Jeff, you and Sergio take the left side, keep your eyes open."

The two nodded and took off as Evan followed Buck to the right.

"Haiden, you good?"

"We're good."

Evan let a chuckle slip as Buck glared at him.

"I heard that," Danica muttered over the line.

By eight, the men started to show for the flight. There would be ten total, including the pilot. He had arrived right after they did to go through his pre-flight procedures.

"Heads up," Danica muttered.

A large gray van appeared and five men got out, bags in tow.

"The three we're missing are there," Evan whispered.

Buck nodded.

The men boarded, and after another thirty minutes, a black car arrived. In only a few minutes, a man emerged with bodyguards.

The man's bags were loaded into the plane as he waited by the car. One of the guards sat at the back of the car while the other kept watch. As they headed to the plane, a swarm of FBI agents took over the airstrip. The men were arrested, and the FBI waved them over.

"Let's go get our guys."

Evan nodded and followed Buck to the plane, the FBI agents holding the pilot at gunpoint. Easing into the plane, he stayed low as a shot flew over his head.

"The FBI has you surrounded. Come out with your hands up." Buck's gruff voice rang out, and Evan shook his head.

These guys weren't going to go easily.

The sound of glass shattering made him smile. Haiden was making a statement.

"Either give up or we'll come in heavy," Evan shouted.

Curses filled the air as he stood and aimed at the man rushing toward him. Dodging a wild punch, he clocked the guy across the jaw and laid him out on the floor, shifting the gun to the groaning man. Buck covered the rest of the cabin, and soon the other men had their hands in the air.

As the FBI loaded the men into their SUVs, Haiden and Danica arrived.

"Thanks for the backup." Evan grinned as Haiden only nodded.

"Figured you would need a little more convincing." Haiden's slow drawl sounded as Danica chuckled and headed toward Buck.

Evan followed and found Buck talking with the FBI.

"We'll meet you. I'd like to be in on the interrogation."

The man in the FBI windbreaker nodded at Buck. "That's fine. But just you."

They all stood at the back of their SUV, loading their weapons.

"I'm headed back to the loft." Danica shoved her hat back on her head.

"I'll go with Buck. I want to know for certain what's going on with Arlo's team." Evan nodded to Danica as the other three followed her to the waiting SUV.

"You're going into interrogation?" Buck's eyebrow raised as he took off his vest and secured his weapon.

"Not into interrogation, I'll watch. Besides, I have something else I need to do."

30

After all the interrogations, Evan was relieved they finally had evidence Arlo was headed out of the country. Although neither Arlo nor one of his known aliases' passports had cleared, the men they captured all told a version of the same story.

Between two hours of questioning and all the evidence against them, the men had spilled their guts. This nightmare seemed to be coming to an end. It wasn't what he wanted. He wanted Arlo behind bars and Bex safe. But if Arlo was leaving, it meant at least some kind of closing of the case.

"Hey, Bex?" Evan knocked on the door, trying to rein in the grin on his face

"Hey." Her smile lit her face, and he felt his heartbeat speed up.

"Hey." Suddenly, his mind blanked.

"Is everything okay? Or did Buck find something for me to work on?" Her eyes twinkled.

"Well, no. We're done with what we had planned for today."

"Oh." She crossed her arms, and her smile vanished.

"But, while I was at the FBI, I managed to get something for you." He pulled her gun from his back waistband.

"You got it back?" Her mouth dropped for a moment before her smile finally came through. "How did you ..." she took it and immediately checked the chamber and the clip.

"They were done processing it." He leaned against the door frame, watching her stare down at the weapon.

"Thanks. I really appreciate you getting it back for me."

He grinned, feeling a pride swell inside him. "What's with the gun, Bex?"

"I ... well, it was my grandfather's gun. My dad taught me how to shoot with it."

"Yeah?" His grin widened as she turned to dig through her bag.

Producing a holster, she pushed the gun in and secured it. "I appreciate it."

Her soft words impacted him, and he inhaled sharply.

"You a good shot?"

She chuckled. "I used to be. Since I changed jobs, I haven't shot in a while."

"I'll take you to the shooting range sometime." He winked as she looked up at him with a grin.

"Yeah, sure." Rolling her eyes, she pulled her phone from her pocket and set it on the desk. "Hey, it's after twelve. How about I spring for lunch for everyone?" She grabbed her wallet from her purse.

"No, you don't need to do that."

"Why not? I've eaten all of your food and drinks. I'm staying here for free, and everyone has had to deal with me." She squeezed his arm as she pushed past him in the doorway, sending fire shooting through his arm at her touch.

"Bexley, it's our job. I don't think you need to buy lunch."

"Someone's buying lunch? Great, I'm starved." Jeff stood at the bottom of the stairwell as Bexley started down.

Evan rushed to her side as she winced, gripping the rail.

"You okay?" He pulled her arm to him and wrapped his other around her waist.

She blew out. "Yeah, going down hurts worse," she mumbled. He helped her reach the bottom and guided her to a barstool.

"Did I hear we're ordering out?" Buck came around the corner, eyeing Evan as he stood there holding her arm. Evan let go.

"Yes, I'm buying. So, what does everyone want?"

The room filled with the whole team, everyone chiming in about what to get.

Settling on an Italian restaurant, she placed the order, reading off everyone's picks.

"I'll go grab it." Evan offered.

"Can I go?"

He looked up to see Bexley watching him intently. "Bex ..."

"It's just down the road, let her get outside." Buck gave her a wink and received a big smile.

Man, how nice would it be to get that smile from her?

"Okay." Evan shook his head.

"Just a minute." Bexley slid from the stool as Danica took her arm, guiding her up the steps.

He started to comment but realized they had twenty minutes before they needed to leave.

As the women disappeared, Buck got everyone's attention. "I finally got something on the bank angle Danica mentioned."

The guys gathered around the island, waiting for good news.

"We couldn't get the names of the account holders, but when we mentioned a possible bank heist of safety deposit boxes, the judge reluctantly signed off on a warrant to get the names of box holders. One name pinged our watch list."

"Lander Karim?" Jeff frowned as he looked over the list.

Buck nodded. "According to Homeland, Arlo and Karim have bad blood between them. Karim is a smuggler by trade but deals in anything black market.

"Apparently, Karim turned on Arlo after a business deal went south. Karim had no idea that Arlo is the worst person to be on the bad side of, so now the theory is Arlo wants revenge. He's willing to do whatever he can to take down Karim. Homeland believes this deposit box could contain names of overseas assets, bank accounts, or other holdings."

"Or information." Haiden chimed in.

"If Karim has information on Arlo, it would be priceless to him. We already learned from the CIA that Arlo's borderline sociopathic and extremely paranoid." Jeff leaned in. "So the bank is the target."

"That's what the C-4 is for. He's going to blow the safe." Evan muttered.

"Now, we don't know this for sure. Remember, the men we talked to today seemed convinced the gig was up. That's why they were moving out." Buck commented, his jaw clenching.

"Buck?" Evan knew a wandering thought when he saw it. Buck withdrew his stare from the opposite wall and turned to Evan.

"Something about that name—it sounds familiar."

"You know him? Karim?"

Buck shrugged. "Not sure. Just sounds like a name I've heard."

Evan shook his head. Buck's career was in and out of so many ops and special situations, names that did pop up usually had meanings.

"I'm still not sold. Arlo could just be trying to rotate everyone out. He's unable to trust anyone. He could've simply thought one of the men was after the money or the information as well, so he paid them to leave. That could be where the money was being siphoned to." Jeff leaned into the bar.

"I'll run it by Homeland and see what they want to do. I told them if it's money Arlo is after, this case is going to them."

"The problem is the small amount of C-4 we found. It was packaged in a barrel, which isn't how it's normally sold. They must've emptied the boxes, packed the barrels, and tossed the cardboard out. We only found one barrel, maybe 25 bricks left inside. So there's got to be more. This is a possible terroristic scenario where he not only busts open the vault and the boxes but detonates a larger bomb as an escape or diversion." Haiden leaned back against the counter with his arms crossed. "I, for one, am not ready to hand it over."

Evan nodded. "Yeah, me either. He's too dangerous and unpredictable. Even if Bex is no longer on his radar and he's just focused on the bank, he's got enough ammo to take out a few city blocks." He motioned to Haiden. "I'm with you. I don't want some other group going in and messing it up. I want us there."

"We can only do so much, gentleman." Buck carried his gaze over the group. "I've fought to keep us on this from the get-go since it became personal with the bomb we found. I'll get this relayed to my contacts, but we're the bottom of the totem pole here. I think they've only let us run with this for so long because they have other interests elsewhere, and Arlo isn't a major target at the moment."

"We got lucky with the mall, Buck. My guess is it won't be that easy next time." Jeff shook his head. "This thing with Bex, I think Evan was right. It was just to keep us guessing. The target is the bank. Homeland needs to understand his intent. Even if they feel it's only speculation at this point, they need to start seeing what we see. The sooner the better."

"I don't know, man."

He looked up to see Sergio's brows furrowed. "What's wrong?"

Sergio leaned over, his finger pointing to a name on the page as he held it out for everyone to see: Bexley Bowers.

"She has a box there too?" Evan watched Jeff huff and start to pace. "What?"

Jeff shrugged. "That's a wrinkle, maybe. He wants her help, remember? It's a strange coincidence."

"I still think it's the bank vault. He's been silent now for a while, and after Bexley talking back to him, making him mad, I can't imagine he actually wants her." Haiden let out a breath after spilling so many words at once.

Evan looked between Haiden and Jeff. "Jeff?"

"The call to her, the message, and now the fact she has an account at the bank. I don't know. It seems ..."

"It's a coincidence," Haiden mumbled.

"Honestly? I don't know. It's a contest to see what he wants more—the information or Bex. But no contact the past few days is strange." Jeff shook his head.

Buck nodded at Jeff. "Let's put our focus on the bank. We have Bex safely here, and there's nothing proving Arlo is still after her. I'll get on the phone and call Homeland, see if we can get any info on his location. We need to be sure to circulate Arlo's picture to that bank branch, make sure they're aware of what could happen if he shows up."

"But the bank is closed off." Evan straightened. "Where would he attack now? What's the next smallest branch?"

Sergio tapped on his tablet. "Looks like there's one on the other side of town. It's in a small shopping center."

"Get them Arlo's picture too."

Jeff shook his head. "Not just that branch. All of them."

"But the boxes from the mall, where did they go? Now that the bank's no longer secure, I'm sure they had to move them somewhere." Evan questioned.

"I'll call the main branch, find out where they've been moved." Sergio pulled out his phone and took a few steps from the island.

Evan leaned back against the counter. All of Arlo's men said he was leaving the country, but this new information was too much to ignore. Arlo's focus had to be on the bank and whatever information it contained.

Arlo hadn't called Bexley or made any other threats. They had checked her home just yesterday to make sure.

So why did he feel a churning in his gut that said this wasn't over yet?

31

Pulling some jeans from her bag, Bexley changed pants and then moved some things around to find a shirt.

"You know, there's a whole closet you could've put your things in and a dresser." Danica frowned.

"Yeah, I started to, I just ..." Bexley straightened from her bag. "This is so overwhelming. Knowing someone is after me, that I'm not free to go do anything ... I just hoped it would be temporary and didn't want to settle in."

"Look, we got some intel today that may point to Arlo fleeing the country."

"Seriously?" She paused and watched Danica a moment, then continued her search. Pulling out a V-neck shirt, she eased the sweatshirt off and slipped the tee on. "So, do you know for sure he's gone?"

Tossing the sweatshirt on the bed, she grabbed her brush to run it through her hair.

"It looks that way, but we haven't flagged any of his known aliases leaving. Until we do, you might consider staying a little while longer." Danica crossed her arms.

"I don't want to wear out my welcome." Grabbing her makeup bag, she headed to the bathroom, and Danica followed.

"You're not wearing out anything. Remember, when you leave, it's just me versus them."

She chuckled. "I'll miss you too, Danica."

After putting on her makeup, she looked for her shoes.

"Have you seen my other tennis shoe?"

"No, just wear these boots, they're cute." Danica was holding the leather boots she packed.

"Oh, well, they're a little dressy, don't you think? I don't even know why I packed them."

"Maybe because the handsome guy who rescued you came to pick you up." Danica feigned a faint onto her bed with a chuckle.

"Yeah, yeah." She seized the boots, trying to hold on to her frown.

"Just wear them. It's wet outside anyway. I guess instead of snow, we're going to get rain this winter." Danica stood and headed for her closet as Bex pulled on the boots

"It's not like this is a date, so stop acting so crazy," she muttered to herself. Standing, she let out a breath, the dull ache still evident in her side.

"Here, wear this." Danica handed her a leather jacket.

"Thanks, but I brought my jacket."

As she reached for the lined jacket hanging on the coat rack, Danica stopped her and put the leather jacket in her hand.

"Just wear it. Matches the boots."

"Why do I get the feeling you're pushing something here?"

"Hey, simply returning the favor."

With a wink, Danica opened the door, and Bexley grabbed her purse as she rushed to follow her out with a groan.

"I've already cleared the air with him, you shouldn't be trying to push," she whispered as she struggled to get the jacket on.

Danica paused and helped her. "I'm not pushing."

"Yeah, right," Bexley mumbled, painfully aware they were being watched.

Danica winked.

"I'm going to get you back, you know." She narrowed her eyes.

LEANING AGAINST THE BAR, Evan hated the idea of taking Bexley out of the office. The danger wasn't over, and getting her outside, even if it was just a few miles down the road, was still a risk. She did seem pretty excited about leaving the house. Danica and Bexley appeared on the landing, whispering back and forth.

"Good grief," he muttered.

Bexley looked way too good in well-fitting jeans with her hair down over her shoulders. He liked seeing it down, and he realized just how much as she turned to descend the steps. She paused as Danica said something and took off back to the room.

Blowing out a breath, he made his way up as Bexley took each step one at a time, gripping the rail.

"Thanks." She sounded a little too breathless as he wrapped an arm around her waist to help steady her down the rest of the stairs.

"Yeah," he managed to mumble as he tried to ignore whatever scent she had on. Was it her hair or perfume? He didn't know, but it smelled great.

"Let me grab my wallet."

She headed to the island and pulled her purse to her shoulder. He turned just in time to see Jeff stifle his grin.

"Thanks for letting me go."

Bexley was speaking to Buck as he ripped his eyes from Jeff, leveling a glare before he did.

"Just stay in the car and do what he says. Can never be too careful." Buck nodded.

"Yeah, thanks." When she turned, her eyes met his and he worked to keep his heartbeat in check. "You ready?"

"Yeah, let's go," he mumbled.

He led her to the back and into the garage, eager to get away from the prying eyes of Jeff and anyone else watching.

Opening her door, he helped her slide into the large SUV, then pushed himself into the driver's side as the garage door slowly retracted.

"You okay?"

"Yeah, why?" He tried to ignore the feeling of her watching as he backed up.

"You're mad at me, aren't you?"

"What?" He paused to look her direction. Her brows knitted together. "Why would you say that?"

She shrugged. "You're just acting strange. And I know you don't want me to leave the house."

"You should be resting."

"I'm just sitting here. You act like I'm going to run a marathon or something."

He tried to hide his amusement at her annoyed tone. "Look, I just think you staying inside where it's safe and restful would be best."

"Danica told me you guys think he's gone."

"We have no confirmation of that. Just because some of his men jumped ship doesn't mean he's going, too."

Telling her about their new theory seemed like a bad idea. After all, it was just a theory.

Glancing her way while stopped at a light, he felt more moving between them. His worry waned as he struggled to pry his eyes away. She sat staring out the window.

"You look nice."

"What? I'm just in jeans and a T-shirt." Her voice came out strained as her head whipped around to see him.

"Just trying to pay you a compliment." He worked a smile as her eyes widened.

"Thanks." That soft voice of hers sent a shiver down his spine.

"You're welcome. And I wasn't kidding about the shooting

Fighter

range, Bex. Once this is all over, I'll take you sometime." He smiled at her chuckle.

"Sure. It's been several months since I even removed it from the holster, but why not? It won't be embarrassing at all."

He laughed and looked her way, finding her pretty green eyes focused on his. "Then I'll just have to re-teach you."

Her cheeks flushed as she turned away.

"I ... I thought the restaurant was just down this street?" She cleared her throat as she gripped her hands and he smiled. Seemed he wasn't the only one feeling it.

"Yeah, but with noon traffic, everyone is on the road." Making himself focus, he gripped the wheel as the rain started coming down in sheets.

Taillights burned bright as they paused and surged at the series of lights. Within a few miles, they were in front of the restaurant.

"Stay here. I'll go get the food."

"Look, there's going to be a lot of bags. I can carry a few."

"It's raining."

"It's just a little water, Evan."

Even though her tone was annoyed, hearing her say his name made him smile. "Okay, fine."

Luckily, the rain had eased to a steady mist. He helped her down from the SUV and gripped her hand as he slowly made it across the parking lot, until she picked up the pace and pulled him under the awning.

"I don't mind a little rain, Ev. But I don't want to stand out in it." She huffed and shook out her hair that had started to curl.

"Why not? You look good all wet." He chuckled as she punched his shoulder. "Easy, no need to be violent." He smiled as she worked to control her smirk.

After a roll of her eyes, she grinned. "Very funny. At least you have a hat to keep the rain off your face."

"Fine, here." He pulled off the hat and set it on her head. *Oh, man.* "That looks good, too." He forced a smile, clearing his throat and turning to open the door to the restaurant. "Let's get the food and get back in the car before the rain picks up again."

She nodded and stepped through as he worked to ease the pounding in his ears. Attraction, heat—whatever this was, it wasn't coming close enough to an end, even after their talk. Even after the Tennison situation. But maybe when it was all over ...

Don't be crazy. She said she didn't even want a relationship at all.

He sighed. But friends—he could do friends, right? Not seeing her every day like he did now—her living in her house instead of the room above his, that could work, right?

Straining to get his mind in gear, he was glad when she took over and requested the large to-go order at the desk. He filled his arms with all but three bags, which she slung on her arms.

"Let me go get the car and I'll pull up."

"It's barely sprinkling, I'll be fine. Besides, I have your hat to keep the rain off my face." She winked and stepped off the curb toward the car.

He followed, unlocking the SUV, and raising the hatch. He helped her pile all the food in the dividers in the back of the SUV. The hatch gave them some relief from the rain as she went through and checked the large order, making sure everything was there.

"I think they got it all."

"Good, because the rain's picking up."

They both stepped back as he shut the hatch and he led her around the SUV. The rain pounded as they pushed into the narrow space between his car and another.

"Evan, hurry up."

He smiled as she leaned into him, trying to keep the rain from pelting her.

"Can you get in?"

The small opening required her to turn and twist and he worried about her side. But she made it in, and he slammed the door. Rushing to the other side, he slid in behind the wheel, then rubbed his hands through his hair.

"You. Are. Soaked." She held her hand over her mouth, trying to hold in her laughter his shirt stuck to his skin. Why didn't he grab his rain jacket earlier?

"If someone didn't have my hat—"

"Oh, no. You gave me the hat. Besides, I don't think it would've helped." Her wide eyes and laughter made him lean on the console toward her. "Why didn't you grab a jacket?"

"I guess I was too distracted." He winked and turned the car on, adjusting the heat.

Although he was soaking wet, with the heat moving between them, he really didn't need the vents.

"Here." She leaned over to push the hat back on his head.

He pulled it off and put it on top of her head, pulling her back to the middle. "It looks much better on you."

Watching her green eyes move rapidly around his face, she finally landed on his eyes.

"Bex, our little talk didn't do much did it?"

"I ... I guess not. But it's all the same, I mean, nothing has changed." She licked her lips and swallowed.

"Right, but I was hoping this might be easier, more just friends."

"We are friends." She flashed a smile and he refrained from leaning forward. "I did want to say something."

He took a breath. "Okay." He found his fingers wrapping around hers as she shifted around in the seat.

"Evan, I never thanked you—"

"Don't." He shook his head.

"Yes, I need to." This time she leaned in, too close. "You've already saved me a few times. You saved my life—that deserves thanks. Thank you."

Her eyes searched his as he gripped the steering wheel, hoping it would keep him from leaning forward and finding out what it would be like to kiss her soft, pink lips. Her hair curled around her face as the wetness from the rain made it stick to her cheeks.

Clearing his throat, he looked away for a moment.

"Evan?"

"Anytime, Bexley." He turned back to see the confusion on her face. "All you have to do is ask, and I'll be there anytime." Squeezing her hand, he let go and backed out of the parking lot, eager to get to the office before his body took over and things got even more out of hand.

32

"So, what's it like to work at a library?" New topic. They could be friends, they could do this. They just had to avoid the awkward silences.

She chuckled. "Boring. But I guess you wouldn't know anything about that, would you?"

He smirked. She was trying again to get some information. Checking his mirrors as traffic stopped at a light, he turned.

"What do you want to know?"

That amazing grin took over her face as she leaned into the middle console. Man.

"I know you're Navy, who did you serve with?"

"SEALs."

She nodded. "Why are you here? You have that military machine drive. I see it in you and Buck."

He chuckled as the traffic started up again. "Yeah, well, my time got cut short."

"What?"

"Injury. Couldn't get back in."

"I'm sorry, Evan. I just—you don't act injured."

He nodded, glancing at the large diesel pick-up truck a few spaces behind them. "I got rocked by a mortar, landed on my right side. Lost most of my hearing in my right ear. Kinda hard to get back in with only one good ear."

Traffic started to slow again as he clenched his jaw. The large truck was moving in fast.

"Hang on, this isn't right."

Slamming on his brakes, his hand went to Bex, gripping her arm.

"Get down, push the seat back and get on the floorboard, now!" He hit the call button on the steering wheel.

"Hey—"

"We need backup!" He didn't wait for Buck to finish his sentence.

A man in a black hoodie jumped from the car in front of him with a semi-automatic rifle. Evan ducked down as bullets splintered the windshield. Gunning the engine, he slammed into the car in front, then shoved the gear in reverse.

"Hang on!" Peering over the wheel, Evan backed up and then swerved into traffic. "You guys on your way?"

"Give us five." Buck's voice called through the speakers as Evan's SUV dodged the cars on the highway, noticing the truck from earlier following him closely.

"You okay?" He looked to Bex.

"I'm not injured if that's what you're asking." She glared up at him from the floorboard, her face red.

"Just stay down, they're still following us."

Rifle fire sounded again as his back glass shattered, and he felt the shift of the SUV.

"They hit the tires. We don't have much time." He gritted his teeth as he floored the accelerator.

He needed to make distance between them before he couldn't control the car anymore.

"Bex, normally I wouldn't do this, but I need you to give me some cover." He started to pull out his back up when she popped up with her handgun.

"Tell me when."

Fighter

He grinned as he focused back on the road. "Take out what you can."

She fired several times and he instinctively glanced in his mirror. Direct hits to the driver's side of the advancing truck.

"I don't think I need to take you shooting," he muttered.

He pushed the SUV forward in the tight traffic. Gripping the wheel, he used the other cars as a blockade and forced the SUV to the right side rail. The diesel truck was too big to fit in the gap that closed after he passed, and he braked.

"Climb out and run, you'll meet the team on the way."

"I'm not leaving—"

"Bex, don't do this again." He pulled her arm toward him, forcing her out his door as he fired on the truck. "Run, now!"

Ducking behind the door, he watched her gripping her side as she sprinted and weaved down the road. Taking a deep breath, he situated himself in front of the SUV, firing as he moved to the next car.

He was pushing them back, closing the gap between him and the team, when a burning pain ripped through his arm. Stifling a curse, he took off again, then paused behind a truck to reload.

Blood seeped through his shirt and trickled down his arm as he shoved the new clip into the gun. The rain was picking up again, pelting his body and blurring his vision.

"Where are you, Haiden," he muttered. *I need more firepower.*

Before he could rotate his gun, a man rounded the truck with a knife. A shock of pain sliced through his arm as the man knocked the gun from his hand.

Blocking the attacker's moves, Evan only landed a few punches before a shot rang out and the attacker fell.

"Finally," he breathed out as he went to a knee.

Buck and Sergio appeared, giving him cover as he made his way back to their truck. Haiden was perched on top, his gun set up, firing on the men.

"Looks like the bank isn't all he's after."

He nodded at Buck, breathing heavily and bent at the waist. "No, I don't think so."

"Your distraction worked. Our men followed her, and we have the exact address now."

Arlo nodded to the man. "Get ready for a breach. I want her with me."

"Sir, are you sure she's necessary? If we—"

"Am I paying you to think or carry out orders?" he growled.

The man only nodded and headed out of the room.

"It's almost over, Bexley. Almost."

33

Pacing the bedroom, Bexley waited, praying fervently that Evan would be okay. Emotions overwhelmed her with each step.

If something happens to him, I'll never forgive myself.

She never should've left him. She could've given him cover, given him a chance to get back with her instead of getting hurt. Seeing him firing at those men as she ran away was the worst feeling.

Once Danica and Jeff returned with her to the house, they heard from Buck. Sergio had taken Evan to the hospital for his wounds. The police had set up a perimeter around the office and she figured after this attack, she'd be swept away by Homeland the second they figured out the attack was meant for her.

Buck had been adamant she stay with Jeff and Danica, but with this attack, things were different. They were all in danger because of her, and she couldn't sit here and take that risk.

Fighting back tears, she paused as voices broke through the closed doors. Stepping out into the hallway, the other team members welcomed Evan back as he only grunted and hustled under the staircase, presumably to his bedroom.

"Thank you, God," she whispered as she felt her body ease.

Back in her room, she collapsed in the chair and waited for Danica to come up and share whatever details she could spare.

She rose at the sound of a knock and was surprised to open the door to Evan, red-faced, his lips a thin line.

"Evan ..."

He shushed her, taking her hand and leading her down the hallway, where he paced a moment by the back stairwell.

"Evan, are you okay? I'm so sorry this happened, I ..." She paused as he only stopped a minute to look at her, shaking his head. "Please talk to me. You always have something to say." She crossed her arms, trying to figure out why he had pulled her from the room but wouldn't speak to her.

His arm was bandaged, and there were several places under his shirt that looked raised, like he had something bandaged there too. He paused and pushed his palms into the wall as she gripped her arms. Taking a deep breath, he shook his head, and she finally found a voice.

"I'm sorry. I should've stayed and helped you. I could've given you cover to get away—"

He cut her off as he quickly turned and pushed into her space, gently easing her into the wall as he kissed her. His hands supported her back and neck, pulling her in. She gripped his waist, then pushed her hand to the front of his shirt where she pulled him down just as he started to back off.

His passion excited her, and she wasn't ready to release him just yet. His lips pressed fully into hers as she struggled to keep up and found herself reveling in the feeling of his embrace.

He finally pulled back, ignoring the grip she had on him as he leaned his head against hers for a moment, his breath heavy.

"I ... I can't do this." He whispered breathlessly.

He turned with a groan, leaving her leaned up against the wall, dazed. She watched him go, disappearing into the darkness of the stairwell.

Fighter

EVAN IGNORED the free weights as he punched the bag in the corner of the weight room. Each hit sent fire up his arm, but he didn't care. He deserved it. Bexley should never have been there. Sure, Buck had been the one to say she could go, but under any other circumstances, he would've just said no.

That's why he had kissed her. He needed this attraction to go away—that's all it was anyway. She was beautiful, and he wasn't the only one who noticed. He just wanted what he couldn't have, and the heat had built up too much between them.

Even after talking about it, they couldn't keep fighting it, right?

Another shot sent his muscles into spasm as exhaustion overtook him and he paused, bending to catch his breath.

Unfortunately, that kiss did more for him than any other woman had ever done. Sure, the intimacy of the situation had other things go through his brain, but for some reason, he didn't feel propelled by that need, that want. But he was feeling much more certainty of a relationship and a future with her.

A future? Could that even happen in real life? In his life?

"You need to lie down before you collapse." Jeff's voice startled Evan back to reality.

"Just relieving some pent-up energy. I could've gotten her killed."

Jeff shook his head. "No, actually, you saved her life. There's a difference."

"She never should've been outside the office," Evan hissed through his clenched teeth, his body shuddering underneath him.

"You can't control every situation, Ev. So man up."

"What's that supposed to mean?" He squared up to Jeff, determined to take out his anger on him, but Jeff just stood there, unflinching.

"You like her. You're upset and scared for her because you like her. I've never seen any two people more fit for each other." Jeff's frown morphed into a smirk and Evan fisted his hands.

"You throw a punch, man, I'll take you down a notch. You're injured and exhausted, you can't hold your own. Back down. Go rest or go talk to her."

Evan shook his head and turned back to the punching bag.

"You know she likes you too, right? It's not like it's rocket science. Anyone that can put up with your attitude and still smile at you like that has feelings for you."

"Just back off, Jeff. You have no idea—"

"That's right. I have no idea what's going on. Look, Evan, you've kept yourself clammed up for so long, it was bound to happen. Someone got through the wall, and now you can't let her go, but you can't let her in, either."

He turned to glare, Jeff's face now a bright red.

"I can promise you something. You walk away or push her away you'll regret it forever. I mean, really, a day won't go by that you won't wish you made a different decision. That she was there and you two were together and you hadn't hurt her."

His breathing was labored as he collapsed on a chair. "You getting personal, man?"

"Actually ... yes." Jeff's jaw clenched as he crossed his arms. "You won't get another chance. Do it now before you really mess things up."

"But we're protecting her, I can't just—"

"Why not?" Jeff stared him down again, smiling now. "There's no rule against it. It's not like we're a protection agency. She can leave at any time. Keep that in mind."

He hung his head as the sound of Jeff leaving echoed.

"God, what are you doing to me?" he whispered and felt way more moving around inside of him than he thought possible for a woman who drove him crazy. A woman who argued to argue, was hard-headed, stubborn, and not willing to give a straight answer to save her life.

A woman he loved intensely.

34

"He'll be fine."

"Really? No offense, but how could you possibly know that? You said you don't know him very well." Bexley stared down at Danica. Her body was shaky as she paced the room.

Explaining the kiss wasn't something she wanted to talk about, even with Danica. But after hearing about the knife wounds and injuries he sustained, she was more than a little worried about Evan's physical health.

"I don't, but guys like him, they don't let things like this keep them down. I've seen it too many times. Buck will have to go head to head with him to make him take a break and let his body heal."

She watched as Danica continued working on the semi-automatic on her desk.

"What's wrong with it?"

"It jammed on me the other day during target practice."

"Did you check the firing pin?"

"Yeah, but the spring's good."

"What about the ejector?"

Danica grinned up at her as she stood next to the desk. "That was my next stop." Danica sat back and studied her a moment.

"What?" Bexley furrowed her brow.

"Do you like being a librarian?"

She chuckled. "Well, it's a job, something I need." She huffed and sat down gingerly, working her body to a more relaxing position.

"What do you want to do?"

"Honestly? I have no idea. I've messed up my life so much ..." she trailed off and focused on the floor, not willing to go into it. "I should never have risked my job. I just—things changed and I had a choice to make. I chose wrong."

"We all do."

She looked up at Danica now avoiding her eyes.

"Would you be willing to train?"

Bexley shrugged. "For what?"

"I don't know, are you willing to learn something new?"

"Well, yeah, if it's something I feel like God is leading me to do. That was the mistake last time, I didn't really stop and think about what God would want for me. Everything went downhill from there."

A knock sounded and Danica went to answer the door as Bexley tried to push up in the chair. Silence spread as the door opened, until she looked up to see Evan standing at the door once again. But this time, he looked calm.

"I'll be downstairs." Danica gave her a smirk before pushing past Evan and to the hallway.

"I don't think you should be here." She strained to stand as he came in and closed the door. "And you definitely shouldn't be closing the door."

"Just—"

"No, no, I won't just wait. Look, we both know it's not a good idea to be in here alone, especially after earlier. So you need to go." Her heart pounded and she felt a panic attack coming on.

"I'm not ... I came to apologize."

"Okay, goodbye." She started past him when he took her fingers. She yanked back, suddenly on alert and stepping back.

Fighter

"Um, let's go talk on the deck." Evan's neck went red as he shoved his hands in his pockets.

"Fine." She managed to get the word out as he opened the door, going first and walking down the hallway.

Following slowly, she eased the pounding in her chest. She hadn't reacted to him like that in a while and she hated that she suddenly felt so incapacitated by her fear. She knew Evan, knew he would never hurt her. But still, being in that room with the door shut and the heat that moved all too well between them, they were looking for trouble.

Standing on the back deck, she noticed the deep-set area protected by the building. From a few feet in, there was no way anyone could see onto the deck. As Evan brought a couple of chairs from the edge, she relaxed.

"Sit down, Bex, before you pass out."

"Are ... are you okay? Danica told me about your injuries." She took in a deep breath as she sat, hoping the conversation would take away some of the awkwardness building between them.

"I'm fine."

She looked up at his chuckle and smiled, her nerves easing away. He looked so different now—calm, collected and clean. She could smell his soap or cologne or whatever he had on, it smelled good.

"I'm really sorry. I should've stepped back and taken a break before I came to see you, and I just couldn't stop. I was worried."

"Worried about me? You were the one injured, not me."

"I know, I just ..." he sighed as he ran his hand through his hair.

Turning his chair to face her, he got close enough to tap her knee with his fingers. "Look, this is going to sound crazy. Honestly, I was blaming myself for being too distracted by you. I never should've even agreed to take you with me in the first place. I wanted you there, I enjoy being around you. But I wasn't paying attention. I should've seen that setup long before we ran into it. I could've got you killed. I'm sorry, Bex."

He worked to avoid her eyes, those pretty cobalt blues flitting around and rarely landing on hers.

"There's nothing to apologize for, Evan," she whispered, her heart hurting at the guilt he felt. "You saved my life again. Thanks."

He shook his head, letting the silence settle between them for a while.

He sighed. "I thought if I kissed you, maybe I could just ignore the attraction."

"What?" She managed a whisper as he chuckled again.

He grinned. "I know, sounds stupid. But I really thought that's all it was, and that maybe that kiss would just help ease the tension between us and I could get back to my job without having you on my mind all the time."

"I'm on your mind?" She leaned to her right, resting her elbow on the armrest and holding her arm to her chest, hoping he didn't notice her sudden nervousness.

"All the time, Bex." He finally looked up, and she melted.

There was the Evan she knew had to be hiding under that tough wall. He looked at her with something she had never seen in anyone else's eyes.

"I care about you a lot. I'm sorry for how I acted." He stared up at her. "I mean, I've been wondering if there was more with you and Tennison, especially after the hospital."

She swallowed hard, barely able to come up with a response.

"He doesn't deserve you."

"You don't know me very well," she whispered.

"Doesn't matter. He's a bully. I can see it in his eyes." He shook his head and looked down as she reached for his fingers.

He took hold quickly and looked back up at her with a grin. "I don't want to walk away from this, but if there's anything going on with you two ..."

"There's not, Evan."

He let out a breath. "Good. But I—I don't want to mess any of this up, except I'm not really good at anything but walking away. I don't think I've had a serious relationship since ... ever." He chuckled.

"But this, this is different. I want to do it right, and that means no more conversations in any bedrooms." His gaze stiffened as his smile vanished. "I don't want you to be afraid of me like that again."

She reminded herself to breathe as she nodded, knowing where he was going with all of this.

"You don't have to, Bexley. You don't have to tell me. But I want to know if it happens. I want to know what I'm doing to put you back in that situation so I won't do it again."

She made herself straighten as she leaned forward a little. "Things were starting to get bad, so I left. The other stuff I told you, the stuff about getting too physical too fast, those things ruined me. I want you to know, I'm not sure if I'll be able to get over that, I just don't know—"

"Stop, I'm not pushing that. I'm more than a little attracted to you, so that's going to be hard for me too. We've both made mistakes in the past. Let's just focus on now. If things one day go that way, we'll talk about it then."

Sadness washed over him as he gently pushed her hair out of her face. "I hate to think he hurt you physically, Bex." He swallowed and found her eyes again. "You're beautiful."

She shook her head. "I'm bruised and broken, Evan. I just, I don't think I can do this—a relationship."

He wiped the tears that had found their way down her cheeks. "Okay, I won't push it," he muttered.

He sighed, and guilt overwhelmed her heart. Suddenly, she wanted nothing more than to build a relationship with the amazing man in front of her. Her fear of messing it all up bit at her.

"I'm sorry ... after ending things with Tennison, all this

craziness, and with all this between us, I'm struggling enough as it is."

He shrugged. "I get it. I'm not going anywhere."

"What?" She watched as the worry drifted from his face.

He chuckled, pulling her hands to his lips and kissing her fingers. "Bex, I've never felt this way, and I don't want you feeling rushed or forced into a relationship. You've got stuff to work out, and I'll be here to help you if you want me here."

"I want you with me. I just—I don't know when I can do more than a friendship." She focused on her hands wrapped up in his. "I don't think you realize I'm messed up." Her whispered words hung in the air.

He scooted closer and wrapped her in a hug. Her face buried into his neck, gently holding her to him as she gripped his arm.

"You're not messed up. Don't say that. You've had a tough past, and things are bad right now. But we're close to finishing this up, I know we are." He pulled back and ran his fingers through her hair with a sigh. "Tell me now if you don't think this is ever going to work. I need to know now." He lifted her chin and rubbed his thumb over her bottom lip, taking a second before dropping his hand.

"I know I want this to work, just not right now."

"Good, because I'm too far in to turn back." He gave her a grin. "I'll be here, okay?"

She found his eyes and smiled as he stood, helping her up and pulling her in.

He held her close and she breathed him in, holding on to his side as she pushed her face into his chest. She felt safe here, like it was the most natural place to be.

"Thanks for understanding. I'm really sorry—"

"Hey." He pulled her back with a grin. "Don't be sorry. I want you feeling better and all healed up with this behind you. As long as you let me be with you for that, I'm good."

She shook her head with a smirk and squeezed him as she leaned back in.

Fighter

"I'm worried about you. Please, can you just keep yourself here for a few more days?"

Her grin surfaced. "Gladly."

He chuckled. "If I had known you would be this compliant, I would've kissed you sooner."

Her face heated. "Evan."

"I'm just playing. But don't think I'm going to forget about that."

She glanced up with a grin. "What? You mean that pent-up high school kiss you gave me and then walked away?"

His face turned red. "I'll remember that, Bex. High school kiss, huh?" He narrowed his eyes as he tugged on the ends of her hair.

She chuckled and gripped her side. "Don't make me laugh."

He laughed and she fought to hold it in, stepping back and punching his shoulder.

"Easy, I was in a knife fight."

"Don't tell me you're going to be all soft now."

His eyes danced as he held her hand. "Maybe, if it'll get me some pity from you." He pulled her in for another gentle hug, and she felt him breathe deep as he kissed her head.

Her body eased as he wrapped her up and she wondered if she was wrong about all of this. It wasn't just attraction and physical want, she needed to be with him. He made her feel ... loved.

Pushing away that thought for a man she had only known for a week, she turned to see everyone crowding at the doors.

"What in the ..." she covered her mouth as everyone grinned behind the glass. "Oh my, they think we—"

"I'll take care of it." His irritation rang through as he started past her.

She gripped his arm. "Don't worry about it. They can think what they want. If you think you can handle it." She turned him around to her. "Come on, help me to the kitchen, I'm hungry."

He took her arm first, then firmly wrapped his arm around her waist.

"How long is it going to take for this to heal?" She gripped her side.

"Months." He chuckled as he helped her to the doors. "But since you're so stubborn, it may take longer."

"Thanks," she mumbled.

Her eye caught sight of a bright reflection in the glass, and she turned in time to see an object flying toward her. The weight of Evan's body pushed into her as they both fell to the ground, the concussive explosion pounding in her head as darkness washed over her.

35

Bexley could only hear ringing, even while calling for Evan. He was lying half on top of her, unmoving. The vibrations of her voice hammered in her throat, but the ringing drowned her voice out.

"Evan?" Finally moving him off her, she held his head as she gently rolled him on his side. "Evan?"

His eyes were shut and glass and debris covered him, blood flowing from somewhere. She couldn't tell where. Touching his head, she found a cut and tried to clean out the glass. Sudden movement caught her eye, and she reached around Evan's waist and felt for his gun at the small of his back.

Pulling it in front to protect her, she fired on the men converging on the deck. Taking out two, she felt around for Evan's phone and started to call for help when a yell made her turn. Shoving the phone in her boot, she fired again but missed. Shouts echoed around her as the gun was struck from her hands and a hood pushed over her head.

"Evan," she called again frantically, reaching out for him as her body was lifted and she felt herself being carried away.

A RINGING MADE Evan's head pound as someone shook him and echoes surrounded him.

"Bex?" Sitting up, Evan realized she wasn't with him. "Bex?"

Groaning, he rolled over and found Jeff, covered in blood and breathing heavily.

"What? What happened?" He watched Jeff's mouth move, but he couldn't hear anything. "Hang on." Shaking his head, he blew out, and finally some sound started making its way through.

"They took her, Ev. I'm sorry."

"What?" Evan jumped up and immediately regretted it as he wavered and leaned.

Jeff helped to steady him. He looked Jeff over. Blood covered his shirt and head.

"You okay?"

Jeff shook his head. "I've been better."

"Who took her?"

"My guess? Arlo and his men. But looks like she got some shots off."

Jeff pointed to two downed figures and a man bound to a chair on the deck, bloody and panting. Finding some strength, Evan pushed himself toward the man.

"Where is she?"

"Who?" The man grinned, teeth stained red as he spat up blood.

Noticing the shoulder wound, Evan took full advantage, pushing hard on the open sore as the man yelled.

"Where is she?"

"Evan, come on. We can't."

Evan spun around and glared at Jeff. "Then leave." He turned his attention back to the man. "Where is she? You don't answer, you'll find yourself with an unfortunate fall off the second story deck."

The man let out a chuckle when Jeff pushed past him, cutting the zip ties to one of the man's hands.

Fear suddenly overcame the man's features. "What? You can't do that."

"Watch me." Evan pushed into the man's face, barely holding back enough to keep from leveling him to the ground.

Another snap echoed as a leg strap was cut.

"You're running out of time." Jeff's even-toned words expressed his understanding as a siren sounded in the distance.

"You don't have much time left, tell me where she is," Evan shouted.

The man paled as Jeff cut the two remaining ties, then pulled him to his feet, wrapping his injured arm behind his back.

"Okay, okay! He's holed up in the basement some luxury condo downtown. That's where he has everything set up." The guy stuttered and swayed, his face twisting with pain.

"If she's not there—"

"She has to be, that's the only place I know of."

Jeff knocked the freed man to the ground only to zip tie his hands and ankles.

"Now we know where to go. Is everyone else okay?"

"I don't know." Jeff looked dazed still, his eyes wide as blood dried to his skin. "We need to get cleaned up first."

Homeland agents arrived and they motioned through the doors, refusing help as they made their way downstairs to see Danica barking out orders.

"You two, come here and sit down." She had donned latex gloves and turned the island into a med station. Sergio sat on a barstool, holding his head.

"You okay?" Evan looked her over, but besides a few cuts, she seemed unscathed.

"Sit down. I know you want to go after her, but we have to stop the bleeding first." She shoved him to a stool and cut off his shirt. "You've got glass everywhere. Hang on."

Evan felt pinpricks and pressure on his back and side as he continued to rip off his shirt. A sharp pull made him wince.

"Sorry, that was a big piece."

He took a few breaths. "Where's Buck?"

"On his way."

He looked over to Sergio, the man's face cut badly. "You need to go to a hospital."

"Just waiting on a ride." Sergio tried to grin but shook his head.

Evan groaned and felt the weight hit him hard. His team, his home, it was all him. "This is my fault. I never should've taken her on the deck, I—"

"Cut it out, Evan." Danica's voice trembled.

"I'm sorry, it's my fault."

"Evan, none of us even considered something like this, so cut it out. Now, go change. Jeff, sit." She shoved him from the stool, and he noticed the tears streaming down her face. As much as Bexley meant to him, she had become important to Danica as well.

Evan headed down the hall to his room, trying to slow his body down before he passed out. Standing in front of his mirror, he closed his eyes as his hands fisted. "God, You can't do this now, not when we just finally got it all together."

He slammed drawers as he pulled out clothes and changed. The cut on his scalp started bleeding, and he washed his head off in the sink. He quickly towel-dried his head and pulled on his boots before heading back to see Danica. "Can you stitch this?"

"Sit."

Buck walked through, a phone to his ear. Shoving the phone in his pocket, he turned. "What happened? Where's Bexley?"

"They sent a rocket through the door. Bex is gone, but the one guy in custody says they're in the basement of some luxury condos downtown." Evan winced as Danica worked. "Where's Haiden?"

"He's already at the hospital."

He noticed her swallow as her hands started to shake.

"You're done."

"Danica, how bad?"

Fighter

She wiped her face after pulling off the gloves. "He ... he pulled me down, shielded me from the glass. He's probably in surgery. There was a lot of glass, and he was out." Her face twisted as she turned to put up her gear.

"Come on, we'll drop you off at the hospital on the way. Where's Sergio?"

"Already headed that way. I'll stay here until Homeland is finished." Jeff nodded to Buck. "Keep me updated."

Evan nodded and pulled Danica by the wrist out the door following Buck.

Once in the car, he shifted nervously in the back seat while Buck barked orders into his phone.

"We'll drop you off at the hospital so you can be there when Haiden wakes up."

"No, I ... I need to be there for Bexley."

"Danica."

"No, I mean, he'll be out for a while. I need to help get Bexley back."

He exhaled and nodded. Searching his pockets, he suddenly realized he didn't remember seeing his phone. "Did you see my phone?"

"No."

It must've fallen out on the deck.

"Let me see yours." He took the phone Danica offered and texted Jeff.

> This is Evan. We're headed to get Bex, go to the hospital so someone can keep up with Sergio and Haiden. Is my phone there?

He waited a moment.

> Okay.
> No, no phone.

"Huh."

"What?"

"Jeff says my phone isn't there."

"Let me see that."

He handed it to her and watched over her shoulder as she went into an app and pulled up his name.

"Wait, you can track me?"

"Don't get all worked up, Evan. We all have the ability to do it on our phones, it's there for situations like this." She kept working for a moment. "That's strange."

"What now?" Buck's voice was more than a little annoyed.

"The app shows Evan's phone moving between towers, toward the other side of town."

"What?" Buck glared from the rearview mirror. "But you said the guy—"

"Yeah, I mean, the guy probably is telling the truth. Jeff mentioned Arlo's need to keep things secret, that he can't trust anyone. But why head there?"

"I'm calling Homeland and see if we can get some backup."

"What about the bank?" Danica shifted to face Evan. "We know Arlo wants that box, right? If he didn't leave the country, then—"

"Then he's after the box. Buck, we've got to alert the bank."

"We sent information to the bank this morning."

"Then call," Evan shouted as he grabbed the phone from Danica. "Where did they move the safe deposit boxes after the mall bomb? That's where Arlo's headed. Does Sergio have that info?"

"I hope Bexley's okay," Danica mumbled as she held her arms.

"He needs her, Dani. Arlo wants her help to get to that box. I can't imagine he has a large crew like last time. Especially now that we've taken a few more out. He needs her without a team to go up against the security."

"Homeland says they'll look into it."

"What?" Evan clenched his fist around the phone. "Buck—"

"I know. Let me call Sergio, I know he was looking into it. Hopefully, the bank will be on alert."

"I'm texting Jeff. He can meet us in case we need him." Danica muttered.

Evan leaned back, trying to breathe as images of earlier flashed through his mind. Bexley with tear-filled eyes, worried she could never be enough for him. But she had no idea that she was who he needed in this life.

No matter how long it took, he would wait her out. Love wasn't a word he had ever used or considered in this life. But now—now he was ready.

God, please don't let me lose her.

36

"Hi, um, I need access to my box. I was told it was moved here." Bexley pasted on a smile as Arlo stood at her back.

"I just need some ID."

She nodded and handed over the driver's license Arlo had waiting for her

"I'm sorry, I'll need a minute. Your box has been flagged, but I'm certain it's just because of what happened at the mall branch."

"Of course." Bexley let out a sigh of relief.

"Come on," Arlo hissed in her ear. "We're going in now."

"You'll draw too much attention," she whispered back.

"Don't forget what happens if we don't get in."

Her jaw tightened as he tapped her lower back. The belt of the bomb strapped to her waist under her shirt ticked away.

He pushed her forward and behind the employees-only desk. The bank manager's office was open, and the teller from the front stood talking to him.

"I'm sorry, you can't be here." The teller set a hand on her hip.

"It's particularly important that I get into my box. I ... I don't think you understand," Bexley pleaded.

A man in a suit and tie walked up. "Marla, is everything okay?"

"Mr. Duncan, these people won't leave."

Mr. Duncan tried to motion them out. "Ma'am, we can't let anyone into their boxes right now. You're going to have to wait in the lobby."

In one move, Arlo had the woman knocked out on the floor and Mr. Duncan at gunpoint.

"You need him!" Bexley grabbed the manager's arm. "We'll need him to get into the vault. If you kill him, we won't get anywhere."

"Fine. Let's go," Arlo sneered. Shutting the door to the office to hide the woman's body, Arlo motioned. "Move." A gun in his back, Mr. Duncan led them down a hallway.

"Marty?"

Arlo fired at the security guard, hitting him in the vest, but the guard went down.

"Don't!" Bexley rushed toward the downed guard, but Arlo shot anyway, killing the man instantly.

"You didn't have to kill him."

Arlo ignored her comments as he shoved her forward along with Marty, who typed in a code, then used a key to unlock the vault.

Once inside, Arlo hit the man across the side of the head with the butt of the gun. Marty slid to the ground, blood trailing down his cheek.

"You okay?" Bexley whispered and Marty nodded with a grimace.

"Five minutes." A voice crackled from the radio at Arlo's side.

"Where is it?" Arlo's words echoed in the large vault.

As his focus went to the boxes, Bexley made her move. From behind, she managed to kick out and drop Arlo to the ground with a scream. Jumping on top, she reached for the gun. With his long arms and torso, he managed to get her off balance, elbowing her in the mouth. She toppled to the floor as he scrambled for the lost weapon.

Forcing herself up, she came face to face with the gun barrel.

"It's not just you I'll kill," he breathlessly gritted out. "Either help me find the box, or I'll kill you then everyone else you care about."

Swallowing the blood pooling in her mouth, she nodded. Her gaze dropped to the frightened bank manager then back to Arlo.

"What number is it?" she whispered.

"4693," Arlo replied.

Ignoring the gun barrel aimed at her head, she knelt down with a grunt in front of Marty, spitting the acrid blood to the side. "We need to find 4693, then we'll leave."

He cut his eyes up to Arlo, then nodded. "Over there, far side near the bottom," Marty mumbled.

She scooted to the opposite end of the large vault, searching the numbers until 4693 appeared. "Give me the keys."

Arlo thrust the metal keys into her waiting hand and she fitted them both into the box, turned them, and opened the cover.

"Move." Arlo shoved her to the ground, then yanked the box free from its spot.

Taking a moment to catch her breath, she pulled at Marty's hand.

"I'm so sorry," she whispered. "You'll be fine."

His eyes closed, his body trembling.

"Let's move."

As she stood, she let out groan and held her aching side. Arlo yanked her by the elbow to the door. "Make sure it's clear."

The hallway empty, she winked at the camera. "It's clear. Where to?"

"Never mind," he mumbled as he shoved her down the hallway and through the fire door.

The alarm blaring, Arlo rammed her into the back seat of a waiting SUV. A large man with a gun sat waiting next to her.

"Drive. I need to study this."

"Yes, sir."

Holding her heavy head, she took a deep breath. *God, help me through this, please.*

37

"She's not here?"

Evan did his best to hold his temper as Buck spoke with the officer.

Even with Bexley's picture out and the bank alerted, she and Arlo had already hit the vault and disappeared.

Jeff and Danica stood to the side, Jeff's arm around Dani's shoulders. Jeff motioned to a man on a gurney, and Evan jogged up.

"Did you see Bexley?"

The man nodded and pulled down the oxygen mask. "She— she saved me. Tried to get away, but the man stopped her." Blood pooled on the side of the man's head, his eyes wide.

Bile burned Evan's throat as he fought to swallow.

"She tried to fight him, but he said something, and she just gave up."

"Bex wouldn't give up," he murmured.

"He said if he'd kill her, then he'd kill everyone else she loves."

"Let's go." The medic pushed the man away to the ambulance.

Clenching his jaw, Evan did his best to focus on the fact she was alive. As he turned to where Buck stood on the phone, his eyes suddenly cut to Evan's.

"Oh no," he muttered.

"We'll be there in five." Buck hung up, his jaw clenched.

"I'm not going anywhere unless Bex is there."

"We need to meet with Homeland."

"Buck—"

"It's classified."

Evan shook his head. "I don't care. Unless Bex is there—"

"It's connected."

Fighting the need to argue, Evan clamped his jaw shut.

"Dani, you and Jeff go check on Haiden and Sergio."

Danica's face dropped. "I'm going with you. I need to be there to help. Haiden ... Sergio said he's on his way to surgery."

"You can't be in the debriefing." Buck squeezed her shoulder. "Jeff, get her safe."

"Yes, sir." Jeff handed Evan a phone. "Backup until we retrieve yours."

"Thanks," Evan mumbled.

Danica pushed into Evan's space, gripping his elbows as she spoke into his chest. "Please call me when you know where she is. She's a good friend, Evan. I don't have so many of those," she whispered.

He wrapped her up in a hug, and she let out a sob.

"We'll get her back, promise." With a nod to Jeff, he let go of Danica and rushed to catch up with Buck.

EVAN WORE a path in the hallway from pacing. He was about to lose his mind waiting when the door opened. Finally.

"Gentlemen."

"Sir." Buck stood and took the man's hand. "Been a while."

The man chuckled. "Too long. How're you doing in the private sector?"

"Normally, pretty good. Today's been a bad day."

The man's smile vanished. "Yes, I heard. Have a seat."

"Evan, this is Senior Officer Hastings with Homeland."

"Sir." Evan nodded and sat down.

"I'm sorry to meet on this kind of occasion, but unfortunately, we're going to have to ask you to stand down."

"What?"

Buck glared from across the table.

"It's more important than you realize that *you* stand down." Officer Hastings scowled at Evan.

Evan narrowed his gaze. "What does that mean? How does this connect to Arlo and Bexley?"

Hastings drew in a breath as his gaze went to Buck.

"We need to know the connection, Bill. Standing down isn't something I'm good at."

"You've never been good at it. Cost you a lot, that bit of stubbornness."

Buck's jaw jumped as Hastings shrugged. "Look, we don't think he knows the connection, but now that we know where Arlo is headed—"

"What? Where is he headed, and why?" Evan stood. "Give me a reason to stay, or I'm leaving now to keep looking."

"Buck."

"I'm with him." Buck shrugged. "You're not helping yourself, Bill. You know my skill set and I'm assuming you know his. We're not some trained civilians with a few years under our belts. We're military-trained agents. Read us in."

Hastings cut his gaze between them. "Fine. But if it leaves this room, you're both paying for it."

38

Bexley pulled at her ties, her long fingers finally getting a hold of the knots.

"It's pointless." Arlo's deep voice echoed in the room. "You know it's pointless, yet you continue to try. Why is that, Bexley?" He stopped right in front of her.

"Call it perseverance," she gritted.

He chuckled. "Yes, I understand. That's why I'm here today. I've persevered, and now I'm within inches of gaining exactly what I want."

"What is that?" She rested her arms with a huff. "Why are you here? Why am I helping you get a deposit box, and why is this bomb still attached to me?"

His jaw clenched a moment, those black eyes burning into her. "I only accepted the help you offered."

She huffed. "Sure, that clears it all up."

He pushed into her space, but this time, she was too tired to be afraid. "That bomb will keep you honest, for now. Just know I can set it off at any time. So getting out of those ropes won't help you, my dear."

Arlo straightened, his eyes narrowing. "Something was taken from me. Someone, actually. I've searched for years, and now, with your help, I've found her. It was always my plan to rescue her. But with your help, I guess I owe you a debt of thanks. Although, I would've had her much sooner had you not interfered."

Bexley's stomach dropped. Someone had escaped his prison and she had helped to put her right back inside.

A clatter sounded outside, and Arlo straightened.

The door opened. A woman entered, tall, with long black hair. She was stunning.

"Arlo Androssier. Somehow I knew you'd make your way back into my life."

39

Evan sat down, leaned into the desk, ready to hear Hastings's story.

"Two years ago, you were involved in an operation to remove a trio of prisoners from overseas."

Evan nodded.

"The compound you raided belonged to Arlo Androssier."

"What?" his jaw dropped.

Hastings glared. "You were sent in to complete a mission, and thanks to you, all three members were safely delivered to the U.S."

"Who are they?" Buck picked up the conversation as Evan stood, pacing the room.

"The woman's name is Isra Hassan. Arlo had imprisoned her and her parents. He claimed to be protecting his future in-laws."

"She was his wife?"

Hastings shook his head at Evan's question. "No, fiancée. Arlo had basically blackmailed her parents, and the only way for all of them to survive was if Isra agreed to marry Arlo. The only thing was—"

"Lander Karim," Buck muttered. "I knew that name sounded familiar." He stood with a huff. "He's our man, isn't he?"

Hastings nodded. "Lander heard about it and confronted Isra. She said she had information pertinent to U.S. operations and would share if we could get her out. Lander became her contact. That's why Arlo went after the bank. Lander had a drop there for Isra."

"Then why didn't you set up shop on that bank? You would've captured him and ended this whole mess." Evan slammed his fist on the desk.

Hastings seemed less than offended as he shrugged. "We had no idea that's where Lander had a drop. Arlo's been in on other business, and we've never been able to deter him. This ... we just didn't expect this."

Evan clamped his jaw closed, fisting his hands. "This could've been avoided, all of it, if Homeland had moved quicker."

"The FBI had the bombing under control, said they had Arlo in their sights. We were keeping tabs, making sure it didn't stray into another incident."

Evan paused in front of Buck. "I'm going. We need eyes."

"You need to stand down. You realize if Arlo figures out who you are, he'll kill this Bexley woman for revenge."

Evan shook his head. "Then he won't figure it out. He wouldn't be able to recognize me from that night."

"Let's go." Buck nodded to Hastings. "Thanks for the heads up, Bill. That lack of communication has cost us all a lot. Nothing's changed with you, either."

"ISRA? IS IT REALLY YOU?"

Bexley's jaw dropped at Arlo's changed demeanor.

"What have you done?" The woman's eyes met Bexley. "Why is she here and tied up?"

Arlo seemed entranced as he ignored Isra's questions. "I've been looking for you for years."

Fighter

"You should've given up. That's why I left, Arlo, so you would give up."

He looked inclined to slap the woman's face, and she stepped into him, bracing for it.

"Don't make me do something I'll regret later, Isra," he muttered. "I've been searching for years, waiting for this moment."

"You're nothing but evil."

Arlo huffed. "Evil? Of course not. I'm careful, intelligent, prepared."

Isra crossed her arms. "Untie that woman."

"You don't understand. She's the reason you're here. If it weren't for her, I'd never have been able to find you."

Isra's eyes cut to Bexley.

"I had no idea. He's been chasing me and kidnapped me and threatened everyone ..." Bexley tried to control the guilt-ridden words falling from her mouth. "I'm so sorry."

Arlo let out an exasperated scoff. "Enough of this. Isra, come with me, and this woman will go free."

Isra scoffed. "I know you much better than that. I've never seen you allow one person to go free once you have a hold of them."

"Then perhaps you should do as I say, or she'll pay the consequences," he seethed. "I've been waiting for this moment for two years. You'll not spoil it for me."

Isra's gaze cut to her for a moment. "Fine. But if anything happens to her, you'll lose more than just me."

Arlo took hold of her elbow and escorted her out of the room.

40

Evan paced the parking lot. "It's going to be a huge challenge to track someone that's an expert at disappearing. How do we find Isra woman?"

Buck leaned against the SUV, holding his chin. "Bexley's smart. She's not in the clear, but I think he'll keep her alive."

Evan paused in front of Buck. "This Lander guy, you know where he is?"

Buck frowned. "No, but I'm sure Homeland has already contacted him."

"I want to know more about that woman and whose side she's on. I lost some men that day. I lost a lot," he muttered. That was his last trip out, the last deployment. The damage done to his hearing had ejected him from his team. He shook his head and pulled out the phone.

"I'll check in."

Dialing rapidly, he called Danica.

"Did you find her?" The hysteria in her voice was unnerving.

"No, but we know the situation a little better. Buck's been making some calls ..."

Her heavy sigh echoed.

"How's Sergio and Haiden?"

"Sergio was released, Haiden's still in recovery. They had ... there was a lot of glass," she whispered.

"He'll make it. He's too tough for that to keep him down."

"Yeah, well, right now I'm more concerned about Bex and what that crazy guy is going to do with her."

He tried to swallow the lump in his throat. "Bex is smart. She'll come up with something. Is my phone on yet?"

They had tracked the signal to an abandoned warehouse, similar to the one they found Bexley in the first time. Then it disappeared.

"No. It must be dead. I can usually activate it if I need to ..." she trailed off. "Call if you find anything."

"Will do."

Shoving the phone in his pocket, he heard Buck's voice echo.

"Then I'm headed that way." Buck hung up and gave him a nod. "Let's go. I think I have a handle on Lander and maybe he'll have an idea where Arlo will land."

Following Buck into the SUV, he leaned back against the seat and prayed.

God, please, please protect her until we get there. Show us the right path.

BEXLEY FINALLY LOOSENED the ropes enough to work her hand free.

It'd been at least an hour since they had left her alone, and she was willing to do just about whatever she could to get loose and out of this building, even with a bomb strapped to her waist.

She pulled at the slack on her other wrist until both hands were free, then searched with tingling fingers for any give in the rope around her ankles. As she finished, a clatter made her jump.

Wrapping the ropes back around her ankles and hand, she gripped the remnants of the rope from her right so it would appear it was still knotted.

Fighter

"I want to see her. Now."

Another clatter, and the door opened. The woman slammed and locked the door, pushing the large bolt in place.

"We don't have much time," the woman murmured as she rushed toward Bexley.

"Don't. Don't get close. He's got a bomb on me."

The woman took in a breath, stepping back to the door. Bexley revealed her freedom and jumped from the chair. Pulling up her shirt, she gave a glimpse of the bomb strapped to her waist.

"I need to get out. Which is the quickest way?"

The woman motioned to her left. "In the hallway, go left and take the last door. It will lead you outside and to the wall. But I'm sure he has men—"

"Not going to be an issue," Bexley mumbled. "Are you staying?"

The woman looked between her and the door. "He will have no trouble finding my parents. He needs to be stopped."

"How do we do that?"

"I ... I don't know."

Bexley searched through the table, looking for anything to help her escape or a weapon.

The sight of a charger made her breath catch. "The phone," she muttered.

Sitting down, she unzipped her boot and tugged it off, the pressure inside making it almost impossible. As she finally yanked it free, Evan's phone fell out.

"Thank you, Lord," she whispered as she hooked it to the charger. "The phone is dead, but if I can get a signal and get a call, my team will come and get us."

"Us? You think they would get both of us?"

"Of course." She shrugged and turned to see Isra leaning against the wall, tears running down her face. "What's wrong?"

"I don't think they'll risk helping me again."

"Again?"

243

A banging on the door made Isra jump.

"Let's go!" Bexley yanked the charger from the wall, slipping her boot back on and heading toward the window.

Using a stool, she managed to get the panel loosened enough to swing out. In the darkness, she swallowed at the expanse in front of her. There was nothing: no trees, no grass or buildings.

Where were they?

41

Buck pulled up to Westin's Club, the high-priced club for the wealthy. One of the many in Dallas, anyway.

Range Rovers and BMWs lined the parking lot. Sliding from the SUV, Evan met Buck at the front of the car, Buck holding his phone to his ear once more.

"Yeah, outside now."

"He here?"

Buck nodded.

Tamping down his need to hit something, Evan paced, waiting once more.

"Mr. Thompson."

A man with bright white teeth and bleach-blond hair extended a hand to Buck.

"Lander."

The man's smile disappeared. "It's actually Foust. Richard Foust. I would prefer you use that name while here in the States."

Buck nodded and motioned toward the sidewalk. "We need to talk."

Foust blew out a deep breath, following Buck's lead. Evan came along behind.

"I figured you would. I've already discussed everything I know with Homeland. I can't give you anything more."

"Try," he mumbled from behind them.

Foust and Buck both turned with a glare.

Evan shook his head, not caring about their brooding stares. "I want information on Arlo and the woman he wants back. Now."

"I don't know where he is."

Buck held up his hand, barely stopping Evan from convincing Foust otherwise. "Look, he's taken a hostage in order to get this woman back. There's an American citizen involved."

Foust looked around. "Arlo is a sociopath who will do whatever it takes to get what he wants. The people you're talking about had levels of information we needed. That's why we brought them here and gave them immunity."

"Then they all need help." Buck leaned in.

Foust let out a breath. "Look, I can't tell you anything about where they are."

"We're not asking about them," Evan seethed.

"I don't know where Arlo is. But I do know a contact of his." Foust shifted, looking past Buck. "His name is Vincent Browning. He lives here in Dallas and has contact with Arlo from time to time. If Arlo is here, hiding out somewhere here, then I bet he contacted Vincent for a place to lay low."

"Thanks." Buck had his phone to his ear, turning to leave Evan to stare at the man that sent him into that place.

"If I can help out, I want him caught. That man will come after me next." Foust shrugged.

"How did he know about the bank?"

"I have no idea." Foust's face went crimson as his jaw clenched. "But when I find out, I plan to take care of it."

"Evan."

He nodded to Foust and turned.

"We've got an address."

He followed Buck into the SUV. "We're going to see Vincent?"

"Didn't have to. Homeland has him in custody."

"What? Something else your friend didn't think we needed to know?" Evan gripped the door, his body tensing.

Buck huffed. "Trust me, not a friend. But he did tell me that Vincent has several warehouses and condemned buildings under an LLC. One sticks out. He recently had the power switched on, and according to SAT footage, there's movement."

Evan breathed deep, trying to calm his heart. "We're going in, right?"

Buck glanced over. "I told him we were. Let's see if we can get there first."

BEXLEY PULLED ISRA BEHIND HER, ducking as yelling erupted from the building.

"They're going to find us," Isra whispered as Bexley shushed her.

"We need to find a place to plug in the phone, then wait them out." Scanning the area, another building across the road appeared lit up. "There, we need to get across the road and into that building."

Soldiers appeared, searching, automatic rifles across their chests.

"You go."

"What?" Bexley turned, pulling on Isra's elbow. "We both go."

"No, we'll never make it together." Isra took a deep breath. "I will distract them. You get help." Tears rolled down her cheeks, she pushed them way with a frown. "He's put enough fear into my life, I will no longer run." Her big brown eyes met Bexley's. "I'll stop him from detonating the bomb, I promise."

"Isra?"

The woman scurried along the brush, hunched down in the ravine. Bexley wanted nothing more than to grab her, but she was right. Without a distraction, she could never get to the other building and get a call out.

Quietly sliding toward the fence, she heard a loud yell. The two men searching had turned and were running to the back of the building.

Bexley jumped up and sprinted to the fence, looking for a hole. Bending back part of the chainlink next to the post, she managed to wiggle through, pausing at the pain shooting through her side. Steeling herself with a breath, she stood and darted to the other side, through the open gate, and started testing doors.

Finding none unlocked, she went to the back and broke out a window to make entry.

Searching the walls, she finally found an outlet and impatiently waited for the phone to charge.

"Come on," she muttered.

Sliding to the floor, she held back her sobs, her side burning as the pressure of the bomb intensified the pain. Her head leaned back, she noticed the flashing red light on the wall. At least the police would be by soon, alerted to the breakin. One way or the other, she was getting help.

"Hang on, Isra." She looked down at her waist and closed her eyes. "God, please give me a chance to get out of this. Again."

42

Evan almost dropped the phone as his name came up on the screen.

"Bex?"

"Listen, I need you to track this phone and get my location. I don't have much time."

"Are you okay?"

"Evan, my location?"

Buck picked up his ringing phone.

"I think Danica already has you locked." Evan turned to see Buck nod.

"Yeah, Dani, she's on with Evan."

Evan blew out a breath. "What happened? Are you okay?"

"I'm hiding across the street from where Arlo has Isra."

"Isra?"

"She's the whole reason ..." Her voice trailed off.

"Bex?" Evan sat up and glanced at Buck.

"We're one minute out. Dani's got everyone coming in," Buck muttered, and Evan could feel the vehicle accelerating.

"Bex?" Silence met his voice. For the next sixty seconds, the only sound he heard was his heartbeat echoing in his ears.

Their vehicle rounded the corner to the sight of two hulking gunmen dragging Bexley across the street by the arms.

He dropped the phone and pulled his Sig, leaning from the window, and took aim.

"Police," Buck shouted from the other side.

Gunshots. Evan took out the man who had released Bex to aim and fire. He took the other out as Buck came to a stop.

Jumping from the truck, he grabbed for Bexley as she got up, backing away.

"Wait! There's a bomb and I ..." She lifted her shirt, and his gut dropped.

"Don't move." He knelt in front of her. "Buck, grab my bag."

"On it."

"You need to get back. Now that he knows you're here—"

"Quiet." He looked up, needing badly to disconnect from her gaze. "I've got this."

Buck dropped the bag next to him, and he pulled out some pliers.

"I've set up the jammer from my phone. It should buy us some time," Buck mumbled from behind Evan.

Searching the wires, Evan separated each one, needing to disconnect it from mobile detonation. Finding the right wire, he snipped it.

"You're good. He can't call it in now. I just need to—"

"You have to get in there, get Isra back," Bex pleaded.

Evan shook his head, sirens drowning out his breathing as Homeland arrived.

"Please, go get her. She ... she sacrificed herself so I could get out."

Clipping the last wire, he slid the belt off, frowning at the lines across her waist where it had sat.

"Let's go." The men around him were loading up and headed for the building.

Buck took the belt, and Evan pulled her trembling body close to his.

Fighter

"Evan, please," she whispered.

Leaning back, he kissed her forehead. and took a deep breath. "Only if you stay here."

Tears streaming down her face, she managed to nod. Opening the SUV's door, he guided her inside. "Stay put."

She nodded, and he kissed her cheek. "I love you, Bexley. I need you to know that," he whispered.

Giving her a wink as she stared up at him wide-eyed, he slammed the door and ran to the back. Buck already had the hatch open and was gearing up. Evan slid on his vest and secured his rifle, following Buck through the hole in the fence.

Homeland already had a firefight going, and gunshots echoed off the buildings within the compound.

"I'm going for the woman."

"I'll follow." Buck nodded and they headed to the far side of the compound.

Using a truck for cover, Evan searched through his scope, looking for any movement.

A door flew open, and he caught a glimpse of a woman straining against a man's arm.

Arlo.

Dropping, he slid along the side of the truck as Buck kept watch from the other end.

"Stop! I'll kill her if you come any closer."

The woman's screams echoed then abruptly ceased. Arlo had his arm around her throat, just like he had Bexley a week ago. But this time, Arlo wasn't as prepared.

Setting up his shot, Evan took a steady breath.

"Tell us what you want," the Homeland agent shouted. But there was no use negotiating—they'd already been down this road.

"Let me leave," Arlo shouted.

"We can't do that!"

The negotiator continued by the book as Evan tried to line up a shot. But at this angle, he would hit the hostage.

In a split second, Arlo shifted, aiming his weapon high, looking to fire on a sniper.

Evan slowly squeezed the trigger. The shot crippled Arlo's arm, and the woman crumpled to the ground. She jumped up, rushing toward Evan.

He lowered his weapon as she fell into him.

"Stop!" Buck's voice echoed as Evan snatched the woman up and hustled behind the truck for cover.

"Isra!"

Evan looked over the hood to see Arlo on the ground, attempting to take hold of his gun. Buck backed up to the truck as Arlo pushed to a knee amid the shouts and warnings of the agents surrounding him.

Locking eyes with Arlo, Evan shook his head. Arlo stood. Blood trailed down the right side of his clothes as his arm hung limp. In a split second, he raised his gun. Shots sounded, and Arlo's body collapsed.

43

Bexley tried to swallow the dry lump in her throat, jumping at every echoing gunshot.

Her body ached, her heart hurt, and all she could think about was Evan's words. He loved her. In all the chaos that made this moment in time, how on earth could that be the only thing she could think about?

"God, please protect Isra, Evan, and Buck. Watch over all the officers and keep them protected," she whispered.

At the sound of crying, she flew from the car and met Evan at the front as he set Isra down. As Bexley wrapped her in a hug, Isra collapsed sobbing.

"You're safe," Bexley whispered.

Bexley looked up to see Evan on guard, rifle aimed over the hood of the SUV toward the building.

"Isra? What did you mean, again?"

The woman eased back, wiping her face and taking deep breaths. "The Americans came two years ago. They helped me and my parents escape Arlo the first time."

Bexley held Isra's trembling hand.

"They saved us."

An ambulance pulled past the SUV as the sounds of boots

echoed around them. Evan knelt, taking hold of Bexley's hand and looking to Isra.

"I'm sorry he got to you again."

Isra's eyes grew wide as she stared at Evan. She straightened and leaned closer. "Your eyes, I remember ..."

Bexley stared up at Evan, his jaw clenching.

"Your voice. You ... You got us out."

"That's classified," he mumbled, winking quickly before standing.

Bexley stood, helping Isra stand as well.

"Isra?"

"Aaron?" Isra took off running, falling into the man's arms.

Bexley looked up to Evan. "Two years ago?"

He nodded and pulled her into an embrace. She went willingly.

"Buck's been talking about adding you to our team."

She leaned back, his cobalt eyes staring right through her.

"I know you could do this job. You'd be amazing at it. I'm not sure I could handle knowing you're always in danger, Bex." He sighed and leaned his forehead to hers. "I almost didn't make it when I woke up," he whispered. "I can't lose you."

She gripped his neck, holding on tight as her emotions let loose. Pain radiated through her side, her stomach.

"Let's get you to the hospital, okay?"

She nodded, not trusting herself to speak.

Evan lifted her, pulling her body in securely, and her eyes closed.

44

"Thanks for calling and checking on me, but I'm good." Bexley smiled into the phone, glad to have Reggie to talk to after being in the hospital for two days.

"I'm glad you're okay, but I'm expecting a call when you head home so I know you're okay. And when I get back, we've got some things to discuss."

Bexley grinned at Evan sitting next to her. "Yes, we do."

"Later, Bex."

"Bye."

"How's Reggie?" Evan took the phone from her hand and set it on the stand.

"She's in London."

Evan nodded, taking up her hand with both of his. "You miss it?"

She shrugged. "Kinda. That career was an anchor for me for a long time. I enjoyed what I did. Even if the clientele was a little snobby." She chuckled as Evan huffed. "But after all this, I think I'm good to go back to my part-time librarian position. At least for now."

"Good to hear."

Two days of sitting in the hospital, letting her body rest and heal, had taken away most of the dizziness and left her side much better. She could finally move around without every muscle in her body spasming.

"How's Haiden?"

"He's awake. Had a visitor earlier."

She grinned. "I guess Danica is keeping him company."

Evan shook his head. "Not Danica. His dad came in."

"That's good." She tilted her head as Evan's jaw clenched. "Is everything okay?"

"Seems to be." Evan squeezed her hand then stood. "Doc said you can go home today."

She sat up. "Then why am I still sitting here? Let's go."

He chuckled and blocked her exit from the bed. "Let me get the nurse and a wheelchair."

"I don't want a wheelchair," she mumbled.

He leaned in and wrapped her up in a hug. Relaxing in his arms, she smiled at the peace that filled her heart. Even though she still wasn't ready for the kind of relationship he was ready for, he'd promise to wait.

And that was all she needed.

45

Evan paced the floor. It had been almost three full weeks since the attack on their office. Parts of the building still needed renovations, but it was the weekend before Thanksgiving. The gala was in full swing, and he was here waiting on Bexley to show.

"Calm down, man. You're making me nervous." Jeff grinned as Evan glared.

"I wouldn't be nervous if one of you idiots would've asked to walk Danica in. Bexley didn't want her to walk in alone, so I have to stand here and wait." Evan frowned at Haiden first, who just looked away, then Jeff.

"Actually, I did."

"What?" Haiden's face went red, and Evan chuckled.

"What did I tell you?" Evan had worked on Haiden to ask Danica to let him escort her for the past three weeks.

But Haiden was too stubborn. He kept saying she would read into it, and he didn't want her to think something more. Well, now it just proved how much she wanted Haiden to ask.

Grumbling, Haiden shoved his hands in his pockets. Working his sleeves, Evan tugged at his collar. They had all agreed to wear their uniforms. There was no way he showing up to this thing in a monkey suit if he could help it.

In fact, Bexley seemed encouraged when she casually asked what he would be wearing. He remembered just part of the conversation he had overheard a month ago standing outside Danica's room as the woman talked. She said something about his uniform and fanning the flames. He was hoping this might be the night he could convince her of something more than friendship. Maybe the uniform would bring him luck.

The last few weeks had been better than any he could remember. Bexley was there at the office, helping out with whatever she could, even with her limited movement. While she was still at the library three days a week, they made it a habit to eat lunch and dinner together every day.

Their friendship was solid, and he had started praying again about what God would want from him as a mate. Because as much as he fought it, he wanted Bexley to be his. Officially, permanently.

That meant he needed to figure out what he needed to do to be better, to be the best man he could be for her. If she ever decided to move on to something more, he was determined to find a way to to help her commit, permanently. It was a plan that could easily fail, and he prayed every day that he wouldn't mess it up.

"You ready for all of this?"

"No, not at all." Bexley exhaled and nervously shifted as she gripped Danica's arm. They stood at the entrance to the ballroom, just inside the outer doors.

"You know, I wouldn't have minded if you came with Evan." Danica grinned as Bexley fought her nerves.

"No, I wanted to come with you."

"You're going to tell him tonight, aren't you?"

Fighter

Bexley's eyes widened as she stared at Danica. "What?"

"That you love him. It's all over your face. It has been for a while, just so you know." Danica chuckled and Bexley rolled her eyes, taking a deep breath.

"Yeah, well, I'm ready to move forward." She grinned as Danica gave her a hug.

"I'm so happy for you, Bex."

"Thanks, I'm happy for me too." She licked her lips as she linked arms with Danica. "Okay, here we go."

"Wow."

Evan turned at Jeff's observation. Bexley entered the room, her arm in Danica's. She wore a navy gown that showed off her arms and figure, making his mouth go dry.

"You are in so much trouble." Jeff's voice barely registered as Evan forced his mouth closed.

Bexley finally saw him, and he grinned as a flush moved across her cheeks. She and Danica worked their way through the crowd to them.

"You look amazing." Evan smiled and pulled at her arm.

"Not so bad yourself." She smirked as she looked him over.

"Danica, you look great too." Evan tore his eyes from Bexley to smile at Danica in her dark green dress.

"Thanks." Danica rolled her eyes, then looked around. "Where's Haiden?"

He turned to find only Jeff behind him. Locking eyes with Jeff, Evan shrugged.

"Let's go sit down." He offered.

"Yes, good idea. My lady." Jeff offered his arm to Danica, and she put on a smile but was obviously disappointed.

"Where did Haiden go?" Bex gripped his arms, and he struggled to keep from pulling her in and kissing her.

"I don't know. Honest, he was just here. Look, he's not going to do anything. She does know that, right?" Evan brushed some hair from her shoulder and grinned at the goosebumps that formed.

"She knows, but that doesn't mean it's going to make things easier." She squeezed his arm and he chuckled. Her glare landed on him.

"Sorry, I just—man, Bexley, you're always a knockout, but tonight ..." he trailed off as her eyes shifted behind him. "Hey," he moved into her vision, and she smiled. "I won't push anything tonight, but if some other guy tries to dance to you or talk to you, we'll have a problem."

She chuckled and shook her head. "Cut it out, Evan."

"Yes, ma'am." He pulled her hand up and kissed it, loving the look on her face as he did so.

"Let's go sit down." She tugged at his hand, and he blew out a breath.

As much as she wanted to think he was playing, he wasn't. Tonight was going to be tougher than he imagined.

46

Sergio and his wife Tamera sat with Jeff and Danica when Evan pulled out her chair.

Bexley sat down, her eyes drifting to Danica. Danica gave her a wink and smile.

"How's it goin', Ev?"

Evan glared at Sergio as he sat down.

"Just fine," he muttered before he took a drink of water.

When he finished, his hand found hers under the table, and she gripped it tightly.

After praying about their situation for weeks and seeing a therapist Jeff had recommended, she knew what she felt was something more than just attraction, something more than a need to make herself feel better. She wanted something real, and Evan was there and had been patiently waiting for her, never forcing her or making her uncomfortable.

He hadn't told her he loved her since the night of her rescue, but he didn't need to. Every time she looked at him, she saw it in his eyes. She just prayed that tonight, he would see it in hers too.

"Where did Haiden go?" Sergio looked around the room.

"He'll show up later," Evan commented as Jeff changed the topic.

The chit-chat lasted for another ten minutes until a gong sounded and everyone found their seats. Haiden suddenly appeared, holding his phone and pushing into the chair between Evan and Jeff.

"Sorry, phone call." He shoved it in his pocket and took a drink of his water, keeping his eyes on the stage in front of him.

Bexley watched Danica turn her chair to watch the stage, completely ignoring Haiden, and she frowned. Evan had insisted nothing would happen between the two. Haiden was confident about their friendship and didn't want anything more. Danica had stated the same thing, but she couldn't help but worry about her friend.

"Stop it, Bex. They can't be pushed together any more than we were."

Her body shivered at the whisper and feel of Evan's breath on her neck. She heard his chuckle and turned to see those dark blue eyes even with hers.

"Cold, Bex?" His arm was already around the back of her chair as his hand gripped her bare shoulder.

"I'm fine, thanks." She winked and squeezed his knee before turning in her chair to try and focus on what the commissioner was saying.

THE SPEECHES DIDN'T last long. The food was delivered, and Evan smiled. As much as he hadn't wanted to come to this stupid gala, he did want to see Bexley all dressed up, and he did want a five-star meal, which Buck had promised him it would be.

He barely listened to the conversation around him as he ate and watched Bexley laugh along with the others. She fit in so well here, with these men and with Danica. They had become like a surrogate family, and Jeff had been right. Once the dust settled and Evan started hanging out with everyone more and more, they welcomed him without questions or speculation.

Fighter

Buck had even mentioned to him again about Bex coming on, and he said it was her decision, not his. Bexley was tough and could learn anything to be part of the team. And being with her during work sounded amazing, getting to see her every day from sunup to sundown. Challenging, maybe, but amazing.

Dessert looked delicious, but he wasn't waiting any longer. Bexley acted differently tonight, touching his arm or leg, joking with him. If Evan didn't know better, he would think she was flirting. He needed some time alone with her.

"I think it's time for a dance." He stood and pulled at her hand.

"You dance, huh?" Bexley grinned as she stood.

"Of course." Evan scoffed as laughter came from the table. "You guys have no idea." He winked and led her to the dance floor as she chuckled.

Pulling her close, he concentrated on each step, remembering what his grandmother taught him and his sisters growing up.

"You're thinking about it too hard."

He found her focus and smiled as she leaned into him, making it easier to tighten his arm around her.

"I don't want to mess it up." He grinned as he leaned his face down next to hers.

"Why do you think you'll mess it up?"

He heard the nervousness in her voice. Maybe he read the signs all wrong, and this was a bad idea.

"Bex? You okay?"

"Yes, why?"

"You sound like there's something on your mind. Don't worry, Bexley. We're good."

"I know that, Evan."

He released her from his arms, spinning her around and making her giggle as he pulled her back in.

"You're really good at this."

He shrugged. "Guess I didn't forget it after all. Just took some relaxing to make it work."

The song ended, and she looked more than a little flushed as they clapped.

"Let's get some air." She grabbed his hand and led him to the side entrance.

"Bex, you're going to freeze." He objected as she pulled him outside, then stood rubbing her arms, looking around the area.

"Tell me what's wrong. And don't say nothing."

She took a deep breath, then stepped into him, pulling him down and kissing him gently. His hands found her waist as she started to pull back, but he held her in place, his forehead against hers.

"Bex?"

"I just—I couldn't wait any longer. I ... I don't want to be just friends, but I don't want to push this."

"Hey, I already told you, I'm not pushing for that." He sighed. "I've been doing my own praying about this too, okay? Let's just let God do this one. I have a terrible track record, and I'm not willing to lose you."

"You're not going to, Evan."

He grinned as a smile lit her face. Lowering his head, Bexley reached up and clasped her hands behind his neck, and he kissed her gently. Her lips tasted amazing, and he found himself wanting more, but he let her lead as she pulled him down closer. It took more than a few moments before she withdrew a step.

Bexley took a deep breath. "That was—"

"Better? I wouldn't want you coming into this relationship thinking I couldn't do better than a pent-up high school kiss." He grinned.

Her hand pulled his, interlacing her fingers through his. "You've been on my mind, Evan."

He smiled, pulling her in for a hug. "You're always on mine. I just, if we're going to do this, we're going to have to be careful."

"Yeah," she responded breathlessly.

"Not just with that. We don't communicate very well, and I don't want to mess things up. You have to tell me stuff, okay? Even if you think it'll upset me or bother me."

"So, that means you're going to talk to me too?" She leaned back with a sweet grin, her finger tracing his jaw.

"I'll do my best. It's not going to come easy. I hope you realize that."

"It's okay, I can deal as long as you're trying."

She settled back into his arms and they started swaying to the music.

"I love you, Bexley."

A shiver moved through her body, and he wrapped his arms around hers. Leaning his face down to her ear, he kissed her temple. "I love you. I just want you to know."

She nodded as goosebumps appeared down her neck and arms.

"Maybe we should go back inside." She looked up at him, and he couldn't believe he was finally holding her, kissing her, and feeling her against him like he had been so impatiently waiting for the past several weeks.

"Not yet." He smiled, forcing his gaze from her lips to her eyes. "I've got the most beautiful woman in my arms, and I want to see what she might have planned." He grinned at her chuckle.

"What makes you think I have anything planned?" That flirty tone of hers nearly did him in.

"Oh, I can just tell. You're at my mercy, Bexley Bowers. You can't resist me."

She laughed out loud, and he caught her hands as she started to pull away. "You sure are full of yourself tonight."

"What's that old saying? Can't resist a man in uniform?" He grinned as she tilted her head to the side and looked him up and down.

"You sure clean up nice." She sighed as her eyes found his again. "Although I was getting used to the beard."

He raised his eyebrows. "Really? Good to know. But the

beard isn't regulation, and I'm in uniform. I will take it into consideration after tonight." He pulled at her hands and held her steady as he kissed her, his fingers tracing her jaw to her neck, his lips pressing into hers as his heart pounded in his ears.

He sighed as she pulled back. Leaning against her forehead, he held her waist tightly.

"You do know all that isn't true, right?"

"What?" She pulled away a little and he caught her gaze.

"You do realize you have the upper hand here. That I can't walk away from you or resist you no matter how hard I try."

"What're you talking about?" She rested her arms on his shoulders as he straightened.

"I don't know what God has planned for this, but I knew once you gave in, I'd be a goner. I'm setting myself up here. I don't like being vulnerable, and I've never been that way before. But right now, that's exactly how I feel." He swallowed hard, surprised he let all that out.

Her wide eyes searched his, her fingers pushing into the back of his neck and through his hair.

"Then we both are, Evan. Not falling into your arms for the past month has been the hardest thing I've ever done. But I think this is going to be harder."

He nodded. "Yeah, much."

The past few weeks had been hard on him too. He wanted to pull her in, hold her, kiss her, give her much more than just platonic support as she dealt with the fallout the past month.

"Why don't we revisit this spot later?" She grinned as she pulled her fingers in between his.

"Anytime, Bex." He winked, leaning in for a quick kiss. "Now I really will have to pound any guy that talks to you or tries to dance with you."

"You're ridiculous, Evan." She chuckled and led him back inside.

The music and conversation flowed around him, but as he

pulled her into his arms for another dance, he heard nothing, saw nothing but her in front of him, smiling at him and holding him tightly. Finally, he had found her, and there was no way he was letting go.

47

"What's your plan, Bex?"

Bexley walked into the living room with the bowl of popcorn and set it on the coffee table. After a wonderful drive and a romantic moonlight kiss, she and Evan had headed back to her place for a movie.

"I don't know. But Buck did talk to me the other day." She narrowed her eyes, hoping to judge his reaction as she sat next to him.

He didn't show a thing as he wiped his mouth. "What did he talk to you about?"

"He wants me on board. But I don't think he's sure where."

"What does *where* mean?"

"Well, I told him your concerns—"

"No, just wait." He sighed. "I shouldn't have said all that. It's your life, your job. I just—that was a highly emotional time, and I should've kept my mouth shut."

She grinned. "Then we talked about my concerns."

"Which are?"

"I don't know if I'm cut out for that kind of job. I mean, I realize training would give me more confidence, but having to be responsible for all of you? I just don't know if that's a job I can handle."

"You can."

"Evan." She sat back on the couch.

"I'm serious. I've seen you in action. You're calm, precise, you don't panic or take on something you can't handle. Well, most of the time." He narrowed his eyes. "With your firearms experience and quick thinking, I think you could train and be an asset."

"But I'm not experienced. That's what this team needs—someone who can step in and step up. You guys have enough on your plate without worrying about a rookie coming in and messing it up. You know, like I did the, well, the second time with the SUV." She made a face, and he chuckled, then sat back with her.

"That's something I don't want to relive."

"Me either." She took a ragged breath and felt his arm go around her instantly, pulling her in. "Thanks."

"Anytime." He gently kissed her forehead. "Look, you said the part-time job was enough to cover expenses, so just take your time and figure out what you want to do."

She met his gaze, and it took more than a little effort to focus on what he was saying as she grinned.

"What's that for?"

That smile of his ... her heart felt like it would burst.

"Nothing, just enjoying the view." Her fingers immediately went to his jaw as she struggled to keep her eyes off his lips. "How did we end up here, Evan?"

He wrapped his arms around her waist. "I think God had a plan that neither of us saw coming."

She nodded, her focus on his freshly shaven jaw. "I ... I was ready to die that day." His jaw clenched under her fingers, and she looked up to find his eyes searching hers. She took a deep breath before continuing. "I told God I had messed up too much, I was too used up and no one would miss me if He wanted to take me. I had come to terms with it." She swallowed as Evan wiped the tears from her cheeks.

"You're definitely not a mess-up, Bexley. And I'm asking you right now never to leave because I would miss you. I need you." He pulled her in and pushed his forehead to hers, his hand holding her face. "I love you, and I ... I can't breathe thinking about losing you."

She felt more than peace moving through her. "You know, what we have between us isn't going to be easy," she whispered. "And we're going to need a lot of help."

He pulled back to look into her eyes with a smirk, wiping her cheeks. "I'm already working on that on my end." He winked.

"I think we need to work on it together. I know my first step after all this was over was going back to church."

"Sounds like a good idea."

She wrapped her arms around his neck, pushing to the side of his face and hugging him tightly. "I love you, Evan," she whispered into his ear.

"You don't have to say that."

She chuckled at the shock on his face as she pulled back. "You think I'm going to say something just because you do? I think we both know that's not going to happen."

His grin spread as he squeezed her waist.

"I've been infatuated with you for a while. You're hard to ignore." She chuckled as his cheeks went red. "But after everything finally settled, I realized I'd been chasing something that couldn't be forced. As much as I want a family, that support and everything, it's not what's right here waiting for me. I do love you, Evan." She swallowed hard and watched as he started to say something, then stopped, furrowing his eyebrows a moment.

"I don't want to disappoint you. I'm going to try my best, but I told you. I've never been that guy." He shook his head and started to pull back, but she pulled him back in.

"Don't even think about walking off. I'm not asking for

perfect. I know I won't be able to give you that. So don't bug out on me yet."

He huffed but his arm found its way around her waist once again. Leaning forward, she gave him a quick kiss, making him grin.

"I guess I found a way to defuse that bad mood." She laughed as his fingers dug their way into her hip, tickling her.

Her laughter increased as she found herself pushed into the couch, Evan gently leaned over the top of her with a grin. He brushed back some hair from her face.

"Bex, come to Thanksgiving with me. I haven't been home in a while, and I think ... I think it would be good for both of us."

She pushed him off and set up. "Really?" Grinning, she watched his smile grow. "You really want me to come?"

"Yes, you mean, do you want to come with me? I figured I would have to beg you." His confusion made her chuckle.

"Evan, I haven't been to a Thanksgiving dinner in a long time. I have a great aunt and some cousins up north, but they never invite me."

"You won't feel uncomfortable?"

"I think it sounds great. Besides, I'm sure I could get some good stories from your family." She winked as he leaned back into the couch with a grunt. "But, I mean, if you're not the relationship guy." She suddenly realized his family might see something different if Evan suddenly showed up with a woman on his arm.

He straightened and gripped her hand. "I've never brought a woman home if that's what you're asking. But I'm fairly sure they won't be assuming anything serious. For now, I think introducing you as my girlfriend will suffice."

"Is that a hard word for you to swallow?" She smirked as his dark blue eyes watched hers and her arms wrapped around his neck once again.

"Not at all. In fact, I think I'm getting used to the idea of being that guy and having you on my arm. Have I told you today how beautiful you are?"

"Evan, I'm in a T-shirt and sweats and my hair is—"

"You're beautiful. Don't ever forget that, Bexley Bowers. I won't let you." He pulled her in and kissed her, holding her cheek. "I love you," he whispered.

"I love you too, Evan." She smiled as he pulled her in again.

God had a plan for this renewed life, and she prayed it would always include Evan Mitchell.

EPILOGUE

"Excuse me?"

Danica turned to see a handsome man in a suit with a smile on his face.

"Yes?"

"Would you mind if I had a dance?" He offered his hand, and without thought, she accepted it.

"Of course." She grinned and allowed him to pull her around the room as the music flowed.

"You are Danica Freeman, aren't you?"

"Why, yes. And you are?"

"Louis Roltz."

She nodded. That name sounded familiar, but she couldn't place it.

"Is this the first time at our gala?"

"It is. My father attends and is a big sponsor for your little team. I wondered what it was all about."

She tried to keep her smile on, but the comment struck her.

"I must say, I am surprised you get so many donations. Especially after last month's fiasco."

She frowned. "What's that supposed to mean?"

"It's just that I've been trying to get my father to stop giving to every single charity he sees. Yours seems dead in the water. I mean, your office was attacked, your team injured and now, you have stacks of medical bills and the cost to repair your office."

"And we caught a known terrorist who was planning terrible things. A simple thank you would suffice." She stopped dancing and ripped her hands from his.

"Homeland brought down that man, not you. Don't try and take credit." Roltz's smile turned into a smirk.

"If you bothered to read their report as I did, you would see they tagged us with the save. Now, you have a nice night." She turned, maneuvering through the crowd back to the table before her mouth wrote a check she couldn't afford to cash.

The music ended and then started up again before she could clear the floor. As she crossed the room, a pull on her hand made her pause.

"I'm really not interested ..." Her eyes went wide as Haiden pulled her close and held her limp arms. "Haiden? What're you doing?"

"Dancing."

His eyes held hers as he moved her smoothly through the crowd. No emotion, no smile, no nothing. Typical.

"But why?"

"What?"

She frowned. "Don't do that. Don't act like you haven't been avoiding me the last few weeks."

"I haven't been avoiding you." His eyebrows furrowed, and she matched his glare. "Fine, I just ... I needed to figure some things out."

"Oh, please." She shook her head and looked around, trying to find someone else to focus on.

Haiden holding her close and in his dress uniform was more than she could deal with right now. She didn't know how he stood up straight with all the medals on his chest.

"It's not about you. Look, waking up in the hospital, you

Fighter

there and then my da—dad showing up," Haiden inhaled. "It was just awkward."

"I didn't think it was awkward." She pursed her lips, frustrated at his sudden need to interact once again. "Let's just forget about it." She released her hands, pushing away and maneuvering through the crowd.

Since leaving the hospital, Haiden had bypassed her whenever they were in the same room. He used to sit next to her, talk with her, he had been a close friend. But now ...

Grabbing her purse from the back of the chair, she headed to the front to leave.

A lone figure caught her eye as she ascended the steps. Louis Roltz stood staring, a deep frown on his face as he watched her pass by.

ABOUT THE AUTHOR

Cindy lives with her husband Garrett in rural Arkansas. They have two children, Conner and Kenzie, and are surrounded by farmland and cattle. With a full-time job, a part-time job and being a mom, carving time for her writing has become an art!

Cindy is a past semifinalist in the American Christian Fiction Writers (ACFW) Genesis award contest with her novel, *Hostage*.

She enjoys writing strong female characters and has a heart for military stories. Her creative streak a mile wide, she dabbles in photography, scrapbooking and anything else that lets her creativity loose!

MORE FROM THE TACTICAL RESPONSE TEAM SERIES

Book Two of the Tactical Response Team (TRT)

Coming May 3, 2022, from Scrivenings Press.

scrivenings.link/tacticalresponseteam

Book Three of the Tactical Response Team (TRT)
Coming November 8, 2022, from Scrivenings Press.
scrivenings.link/tacticalresponseteam

ALSO BY CINDY BONDS

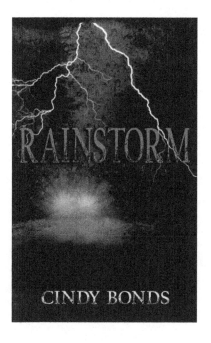

Rainstorm

by Cindy Bonds

Laurel Ashburn has a scarred past, filled with corruption and pain. After an injury overseas sends her home, she moves back in with her foster mother and to a town that hates her. Being home puts her on a path to find a missing friend. But when she's attacked over and over, who will be willing to help?

Detective Dev Hollister traded in the big city for a slower pace and less crime in rural Arkansas. After rescuing Laurel from an attempted kidnapping, he finds himself intrigued with this headstrong and stubborn woman.

While Dev's job is to protect Laurel, he wants much more than to solve the case. He wants to give her a new life and reason to stay.

Laurel will have to push beyond her dark past to trust Dev with her life. But after losing so much, can Laurel survive one more storm?

Hostage

by Cindy Bonds

Her confidence shot, Agent Macy Packer desperately wants to go back to her regular life, before she was taken hostage. To forget the pain, the fear and forget the man that helped her through all of it, then disappeared.

Kane Bledsoe is finally healed, his scars serving as a reminder of his time in captivity. But all he can think about is the blue-eyed woman that saved him. She had saved them all and left him with a burning hope.

A chance meeting and an attack prove Macy is still in danger. Kane pushes himself into the investigation, doing what he can to provide protection.

The enemy is clear, he wants Macy.

Kane will have to decide just how far he's willing to go to protect her. Can he sacrifice himself when the time comes?

MORE ROMANTIC SUSPENSE FROM SCRIVENINGS PRESS

Silence Can Be Deadly

Trouble in Pleasant Valley

Book Three

It started with a taxi ride ... or did it?

Forced from the career he loved and into driving a taxi, Peter Grace had grown accustomed to his simple life. Until one night when a suspicious fare and a traffic jam blew it all apart, and he was on the run again. Only this time it wasn't a matter of changing occupations but of life and death.

He needed help and he knew where to find it. His old friend Rafe in Pleasant Valley. What he didn't count on was finding not only the help he needed but a community of new friends and the love of his life. Zoe Poole.

The story of Captain Nate Zuberi and his wife Madison continues as they too risk their lives to help Peter. Along with Peter, Rafe, and Zoe, they strive to catch an assassin.

But can the group of friends find the killer before anyone else gets hurt?

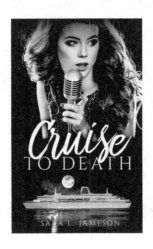

Cruise to Death

Sara L. Jameson

Winner of the 2020 Scrivenings Press Get Pubbed Contest!

When opera singer Riley Williams agrees to sub as a musical-theater performer on a luxury Rhine/Moselle River boat cruise, she gets more than she bargained for. Not only does she have to come up with 250 Broadway songs, she must dance with the male passengers. Dance—the subject she nearly failed in her conservatory courses, and the cause of her recent flop in an opera house. To make matters worse, she overhears two terrorists at a café in Antwerp, Belgium, discussing the transfer of deadly Agent X to the highest bioterrorist bidders.

Interpol Agent Jacob Coulter, an anti-terrorism desk analyst in Brussels, Belgium, insists on serving as an undercover agent after his best friend Noel is murdered by terrorists from the cell he infiltrated in Brussels. Shortly before Noel dies, he manages to tell Jacob snippets of the terrorists' plans. Plans that seem to involve the same river boat cruise Riley is on.

When Interpol learns of Riley's encounter with terrorists at the café, Jacob's supervisor insists he work with her to identify the terrorists and retrieve Agent X. But their relationship is fraught with distrust because of Riley's suspicious past and a romantic attraction neither of them wants.

Stay up-to-date on your favorite books and authors with our free e-newsletters.

ScriveningsPress.com

Made in United States
Orlando, FL
20 March 2023

31242314R10161